SiMON

DODGER FOR SALE

Jordan Sonnenblick

Feiwel and Friends
New York

A FEIWEL AND FRIENDS BOOK
An Imprint of Macmillan

DODGER FOR SALE. Copyright © 2010 by Jordan Sonnenblick. All rights reserved.
Distributed in Canada by H.B. Fenn and Company, Ltd. Printed in April 2010 in the
United States of America by R. R. Donnelley & Sons Company, Harrisonburg, Virginia.
For information, address Feiwel and Friends, 175 Fifth Avenue, New York, N.Y. 10010.

Library of Congress Cataloging-in-Publication Data

Sonnenblick, Jordan.
Dodger for sale / Jordan Sonnenblick. — 1st ed.
p. cm.
Summary: A school project helps fifth-grader Willie, his friend Elizabeth,
and even his meddlesome younger sister Amy, aided by the irrepressible
genie Dodger, save the local forest from ruthless developers.
ISBN 978-0-312-37795-3
[1. Genies—Fiction. 2. Schools—Fiction. 3. Conservation of natural resources—
Fiction. 4. Humorous stories.] I. Title.
PZ7.S6984Doi 2010
[Fic]—dc22
2009048796

Book design by Barbara Grzeslo

Feiwel and Friends logo designed by Filomena Tuosto

First Edition: 2010

10 9 8 7 6 5 4 3 2 1

www.feiwelandfriends.com

To Alexa and Ben.
Who knew being a godparent
would be so much fun?

DODGER FOR SALE

Look, if I'm going to tell you **everything** that happened with Dodger's strange transformations, Amy's disappearance, and our secret battle with the dreaded leprechauns, you have to promise **you won't tell**. And you won't get totally grossed out— even by the parts that are completely **disgusting**. And you won't mention this to any leprechauns you might run into.

Not that I'm afraid of leprechauns or anything.

Anyway, I guess I'll have to trust you on this, right? Plus, I'm busting to tell somebody about it. **So here goes . . .**

CHAPTER ONE

Whoopsie!

I'M STANDING AT THE TOP of a cliff. Well, according to the hand-lettered sign at the edge, it's technically a ski slope. But it looks pretty darn cliff-like to me. I have a snowboard attached to my feet, about a hundred pounds of hot, sweaty clothing on my body, and a pair of goggles strapped on over my glasses so I can't really see where the heck I'm going.

And there's a hyperactive blue chimp standing next to me. Despite the cold, he's sporting nothing but a pair of bright orange surf shorts and a black eye patch. And he's pretty excited. "Dude," he exclaims, "you OWN this slope! This is going to be so great!

3

Just remember, you've gotta BE the board. That's all you need to know—just BE the board. Oh, and don't fall and die. Because that would, like, totally ruin the plan."

I smile weakly at him. "The plan?" I ask.

"You know, bud. The *plan*. Step One: Totally carve up the top part of this slope. Step Two: Conquer the giant slalom course in the middle of the slope. Step Three . . . um . . . I told you about Step Three, right?"

"Is that the part where I get carried away on a stretcher?"

"No, Willie, that's Step Four. Just kiddin'! Actually, Step Three is the ski jump."

"SKI JUMP??? Dodger, you never told me there would be a ski jump! Are you crazy? I've never even tried snowboarding before, and now you expect me to go off of some gigantic ramp?"

"Dude, calm down. It's no biggie, okay? Everything's taken care of. See, we, um, fixed your board."

"What do you mean, you *fixed* my board? And who's 'we'?"

"The board is just a regular, ordinary snowboard, except the bottom has been painted with some—well, some special stuff. And never mind the 'we' thing."

"Special stuff? What kind of special stuff?"

Dodger gave me one of his patented one-eyed winks and said, "I came up with the formula myself . . . mostly. It's the same stuff that's on the bottom of the Magic Carpet of Khartoum. It should give you a little extra lift. At least, I'm pretty sure."

Oh, boy. The Magic Carpet of Khartoum is an actual, real-life flying carpet. And it's not very easy to control—trust me. So I can only imagine the kind of massive damage I can do when I try to combine flying with snowboarding. "Dodger," I say, "this is insane! Can you tell me again why I'm doing it?"

Dodger puts his hands on his hips and glares at me in exasperation. "Dude, do you want to save your little sister from the leprechauns or don't you?"

My life gets really complicated sometimes. This is one of those times. "Of course I want to save Amy! I just don't understand why we can't walk over to their field and ask them to give her back."

"Because that's exactly what they'll be expecting! Duh, do I have to think of everything around here?"

"Okay, I can see why we have to take the leprechauns by surprise. But why do I need to do the slalom course and everything?"

" 'Cause, dude, it's cool! You never need a *reason* to be cool! Now, let's go over this one more time: Do you have your goggles?"

"Um, yeah. You're looking at me wearing them, aren't you?"

"Dude, you're just supposed to say, 'Check!' "

"Why?"

" 'Cause it sounds awesome! Now, let's try again—we're running out of time! Goggles?"

"Check."

"Gloves?"

"Check."

"Map?"

"What map?"

"Oh, oops. Well, never mind that now. Alrighty, then—we'd better get moving! Any last questions?"

"Yeah! Where's Lizzie?" Lizzie is my best friend. And back then, she was also the only other person I knew who could see Dodger. He was totally invisible to everyone else.

Long story.

"Don't worry. She'll be there when it all goes down."

"When *what* all goes down?"

Just then something started beeping really, really loudly. I looked around, but the noise seemed to be coming from the side of Dodger's shorts. He reached into his pocket and pulled out something that looked like a cross between a cell phone, a GPS device, and a banana. Sure enough, it was the source of the beeps. It was also blinking bright orange once every few seconds. "Holy cow!" Dodger said. "Team Alpha is already in position! We've got to boogie!"

"We?"

"Yeah, we! You didn't think I was going to let you have all this fun by yourself, did you?"

"But . . . but . . . you don't have a snowboard!"

"Whoopsie. I knew I was forgetting *something*."

"Wait, so what are we going to do now?"

Dodger took maybe ten steps backward up the hill and said, "We are going to *fly*!" Then he charged toward me, leaped in the air, and landed on the board so his feet were right next to mine and his arms were around my waist. We started zooming down the hill. That was when it occurred to me that I wasn't wearing a helmet.

"Cowabunga!" Dodger shouted in my ear. Then he laughed.

7

CHAPTER TWO

Great, Now I Have to Go on a Quest

TO TELL YOU THE TRUTH, this entire situation was my dad's fault. If not for him and the dumb old self-help books he writes for a living, the whole crisis with the woods never would have happened. I wouldn't have made my New Year's resolution, James Beeks wouldn't have betrayed the student council, and Amy wouldn't have been snatched by the sprites of the forest.

It all started on January 1, when Dad woke up the whole family with a huge grin on his face. It was only seven AM, and we had all been up past midnight, but I guess he was so excited about his daffy idea that he just couldn't wait for all of us to wake up on our own. Amy, my mother, and I staggered downstairs to the kitchen while Dad ran to the hall closet. When he came back, he was carrying wrapped gifts. I know you're supposed to be excited when you get a present, but we were all so tired that all we did was maybe yawn a bit less and try to open our eyes past halfway.

Dad gave each of us a package. From the instant he put it in my hands, I knew it was a book. I usually love books, so if it hadn't been so early, I might have actually been eager to open it. On the other hand, if I had known what was coming, I would have grabbed a pack of matches from the cabinet next to the sink and lit the wrapping paper on fire.

Dad was practically jumping up and down as we started unwrapping the gifts. I don't know why— they had to be the lamest presents ever. I recognized mine as soon as I saw a corner of the cover. I peeked at my mom and sister, and they looked the way I felt. My father had given each of us a different one of the books he had written. As if we didn't already have multiple copies of every single one of his books all over the house.

Mom's present was Dad's first bestseller, *Let Them Play: Allowing Your Children to Express Their*

Independence. Amy's was *You Go, Girl: A Preteen's Guide to Standing Up for Your Rights.* Mine was *Kid on a Quest: Be Your Own Hero (Teen Edition).*

"Um, Dad?" Amy said. "Why did you wake us up at the crack of dawn to give us books we already had?" I had another question: Why in the world did Dad think Amy needed a book to teach her to speak up?

"Good question, Amy!" Apparently, Dad had been spending his free time studying his classic work, *1,001 Compliments for Every Occasion.* "Fortunately, your beloved father has prepared an answer for you!" *Ugh*, I thought. *Dads can be so corny.* "I gave each of you one of those books so that you can help me with my New Year's resolution. You are all going to spend the next six months helping me write a book about my books!"

"Huh?" we all asked at the same time.

"Well, my next book is going to be sort of a . . . a living experiment. My plan is to have each of you follow one of my books as a New Year's resolution of your own. Then I'll write the book about what happens."

"So," Mom said, "it's kind of like a reality TV show, only with books?"

Dad nodded, looking very pleased with himself.

"And you want us to be your guinea pigs?"

"Actually, I was thinking of you more as . . . uh . . . test pilots." I think Dad had also brushed up on another of his books, *Flattery Will Get You Everywhere!* "What do you think, kids? Will this be fun, or what?"

Amy and I must not have looked overjoyed enough, because Dad added, "Oh, come on, guys! You're always asking me to write a book about you. So here's your big chance."

I glanced over at Amy and saw she was starting to smile back at Dad. I had to admit my father was pretty slick. I mean, what seven-year-old girl *doesn't* dream of being famous? I was sure Mom wouldn't fall for it—but when I peeked over at her, she was gazing adoringly at her husband.

Oh, gak, I thought. *Is Mom really that gullible?*

"You're right, honey," she said. "This is a great idea!" Dad's face broke into an even bigger grin. Then Mom continued, "And I know just the right book for *you* to follow!"

Dad's smile got a lot smaller. "For me to follow? But . . . but . . . I'm the one who has to write the book at the end! I shouldn't have to . . . I mean, it wouldn't be fair if . . . can't I just . . . oh, fine. What book do you have in mind, dear?"

Mom disappeared into the living room but was back in a flash. She handed Dad his book: *The Helpful Husband: 101 Tips for Manly Housekeeping*. I should have known Mom would have a trick or two up her sleeve.

I cleared my throat. "Dad? What about me? What's this quest I'm supposed to do?"

"Well, son, I can't tell you that. The whole point of the book is that you need to figure out your own quest. Set a goal! Find a problem and solve it! Blaze a new trail! Make the world a better place! Prove that Willie Ryan can make a difference! And, um, take good notes—that will make my job a lot easier at the end."

I groaned.

Dad looked around at all of us. "So what do you say, family? Are you in? Can we all work together and have a bestselling adventure?"

Mom and Amy said YES! so loudly that I don't think Dad even noticed when I didn't cheer right along with them.

I spent the rest of the vacation worrying about my assignment. I mean, I was just one little fifth grader in one little town. I wasn't even a particularly smart, talented, or cool fifth grader. How was I supposed to go on a heroic quest to make the world a better place—a quest that would be interesting enough for my dad to write a book about it?

On the last day of the break, I went over to Lizzie's house to work on an extra-credit poster project we had signed up to do for our teacher, Mrs. Starsky. It was a crazy assignment: You had to color in a map of the fifty states using only four different colors without ever having two states of the same color touching each other. Sounds easy, right? But it's actually quite hard to do.

Especially when your partner keeps arguing about everything, and a magical blue chimp won't stop throwing crayons around the room.

After a couple of hours, we had figured everything out, except for how to keep Dodger entertained. He had already done just about everything you can do with crayons. He had tried coloring with them, tasting them, melting them on top of the radiator, and lobbing them at us while we tried to work. While

Lizzie and I chatted and colored in the last few states, Dodger decided it was time to work on his crayon-juggling skills. It was a fairly weird conversation.

LIZZIE: So, Willie, I think I've come up with a perfect new nickname for you.

DODGER: Wow, the blue crayon definitely flies better than these other ones! I bet I can juggle three blue crayons with just one hand.

ME: Lizzie, I don't need a nickname.

LIZZIE: But this one is adorable! I think I shall call you—

(Insert crashing sound here)

DODGER: Well, maybe I can't juggle *three* blue crayons with one hand. I guess I should try two first. Plus this glass of chocolate milk.

LIZZIE: Willers!

ME: Willers? *Willers?* It sounds like, um, never mind.

LIZZIE: What does it sound like?

ME: Nothing. I just don't like it, okay?

(Truthfully, it sounded like the kind of nickname a girl would make up for her boyfriend. And I would die if the kids at school—especially James Beeks— heard her call me that.)

DODGER: I don't know, I think it's a cool name. Willers . . . I like it! In fact, that's what we used to call that guy in England who asked Rodger for help re-writing his plays. And he was a cool dude. Well, ex-cept for those dorky shirts with the ruffly collars he used to wear.

LIZZIE: Dodger, are you trying to tell me that Rodger helped William Shakespeare write his plays?

DODGER: Yeah, Rodger just polished up a few lines here and there. 'Cause old Willers would be all like, "Romeo, ah, Romeo, what's up with your name?" And Rodger would go, "O Romeo, Romeo! Where-fore art thou Romeo?" Or Willers would go, "The path of true love was always kind of . . . uh, bumpy." So Rodger would be all, "The course of true love never did run smooth." Or Willers would say, "To exist or not so much? Because I'm wondering." So Rodger would go, "To be or not to—"

(Insert crashing and splashing sounds here) Whoopsie. *That's* going to leave a mark. Anyway—

ME: Wait a minute!

LIZZIE: Yes, Willers?

ME: I don't want to be called—

DODGER: Hmm . . . maybe if I juggled just one blue crayon and this piggy bank it would—

(Insert crashing sound here)

LIZZIE: Dodger, now look what you've done! Willers, could you get a—

ME: Don't call me Willers!

LIZZIE: Could you just be a dear and get some paper towels, please? Before my ceiling is stained forever?

(I run downstairs, get the paper towels, and run back up.)

LIZZIE and DODGER together: Thanks, Willers!

ME: (*Sigh.*) By the way, did I tell you guys my dad ordered me to go on a quest?

LIZZIE: A quest? What kind of quest? Do you need to find an ancient treasure?

DODGER: Fight a dragon?

LIZZIE: (fluttering her eyebrows) Win the hand of a beautiful young maiden?

ME: (blushing) No, nothing like that. I just have to change the world.

DODGER: Well, if that's all . . . why don't you just, like, help a little kid cross the street?

LIZZIE: Or build a house for a starving family in India?

DODGER: Or get the student council to do something really important?

ME: Like what?

DODGER: Dude, I don't know. But I'm not the kid they elected president—you are.

ME: Well, I guess maybe we could come up with something. Like a bake sale. Or a charity bingo game. Or—

LIZZIE: I'VE GOT IT!

ME: Got it? Got what?

LIZZIE: You'll see, Willers. You'll see!

DODGER: Hey, look! I can totally juggle these four crayons and this can of spray paint!

(Insert crashing, spraying sounds here) Well, except for the paint. *How* many colors were supposed to be on this map again?

CHAPTER THREE

Lizzie's Big Idea

FOR THE NEXT WEEK, I bugged Lizzie to tell me what her big plan was. She wouldn't crack, though. She just kept telling me I'd find out at the next student council meeting. By the time the meeting rolled around, I was just dying to know what she was thinking. I called the student council to order by banging this wooden hammer thing called a gavel on the table—which, truthfully, is the most fun part of being the president.

Sometimes, when I'm feeling really wild, I even bang it twice.

Anyway, as soon as the meeting started, Lizzie took over. That happens a lot. She raised her hand,

and when I called on her, she said, "Attention, everyone! I have a big announcement to make."

Mrs. Starsky, our teacher and advisor, said, "What is it, Lizzie? I'm always excited to hear your ideas. They're so new and fresh!"

My archenemy, James Beeks, who had run against me for president and lost, muttered to his friend Craig Flynn, "Of course her ideas are new—until this year, nobody was dumb enough to vote for her." I gave him a dirty look. Technically, he and Craig shouldn't even have been on the council, but Beeks had convinced Mrs. Starsky that with a new president and vice president, the group needed a couple of experienced fifth graders around to provide "balance." So far, all Beeks had provided was obnoxious comments.

Lizzie said, "You know how the student council does something to help the community every year?"

Mrs. Starsky beamed at Lizzie and said, "Of course. You know my motto: Think globally, act locally!"

"Uh, right. Anyway, this year I think we should do something different . . . something to help the environment right here in our town."

A little first-grade girl raised her hand and said, "Hey, we could make it rain more! My dad's a farmer, and he says we need more rain!"

A second-grade boy turned to her and said, "How are we supposed to make it rain? Duh!"

A kindergarten boy said, "I know! Maybe we could save some fur seals! My mom says they're almost a stink!"

Mrs. Starsky said, "That's a sweet idea, Tyler. But I think your mother means 'extinct.' That's the word for when all the members of a species have died."

The little boy said, "Because they smell so bad?"

Mrs. Starsky shook her head and replied, "No, being extinct has nothing to do with smelling bad."

"But," Tyler fired back, "everything that's dead smells bad!"

Lizzie interrupted by saying, "Thank you for sharing your idea—and your interesting logic—with us, Tyler. Unfortunately, though, Mrs. Starsky is right: We need to act locally. And there aren't any fur seals around here, are there?"

"Oh, no," Tyler said. "We're too late! They're already a stink!"

Lizzie put her head in her hands. Mrs. Starsky

asked, "Do we have any other ideas for helping our *local* environment?"

A second grader raised his hand and said, "Mrs. Starsky, Mrs. Starsky! I just lost a tooth!"

Honestly, the next time somebody tries to get me to run for student council, I might just join the circus instead. The kid ran to the water fountain while Beeks snickered, "Wow, Willie and Lizzie sure do know how to run a smooth meeting—*not!*"

Lizzie sat straight up, glared at Beeks, and said, "That's it! Time for a field trip, everyone! Grab your coats and follow me!"

Everyone looked totally confused, but they put on their jackets, and when Lizzie started walking out of the classroom, the whole student council trooped along behind her. I looked at Mrs. Starsky, who raised an eyebrow as if to say, *What's this all about?* I shrugged, because honestly, I had no idea.

Meanwhile, Tyler had started crying over the imaginary dead fur seals of our little town, the tooth kid was running around trying to gross everyone out with his bloody molar, and Beeks was smirking. I heard him say, "*This* ought to be good!"

I was kind of thinking the same thing.

Lizzie marched out the front door of the school,

turned right, and cut diagonally through the play-ground. We passed the slides where Lizzie and I had eavesdropped on Beeks and Flynn, and the baseball field where I had almost saved my team's fall season. Then we reached the sidewalk that runs along the edge of the woods. Mrs. Starsky said, "Lizzie, I'm afraid I have to ask you where we're going. I'm not supposed to be taking you off school grounds without signed permission slips, and—"

Lizzie stopped walking so suddenly that I banged right into her. "That's okay, Mrs. Starsky. We're here!"

I spat out a strand of Lizzie's hair and said, "What do you mean, we're here?"

"Yeah," Beeks said. "What are you talking about?"

Lizzie pointed to a sign attached to a wooden spike in the ground. All the sign had on it was a phone number and two words:

FOR SALE

I gulped. Jeepers. Our woods were for sale? Dodger's magical home? The Field of Dreams? See, these woods are kind of enchanted. If you have a certain kind of vision, and a certain kind of strange luck, you can find a field in the middle of the woods where everything is blue and nearly anything can happen. Dodger kind of hangs out there when he's not in his lamp or following me around. Long story.

This was so not good.

Lizzie said, "*This* is what I'm talking about. These lovely woods—the only green space for miles around—are for sale. And do you know what happens when a forest gets sold?"

Beeks said, "Somebody makes some money?"

Tyler said, "All the fur seals die?"

Flynn said, "A mall gets built right behind our school? With a food court and everything? Because that would be totally cool!"

Lizzie sighed. "What happens," she grumbled, "is that the trees get chopped down, the land gets bulldozed flat, all the wildlife gets either killed or chased away, and we get a bunch of new stores or rows and rows of identical houses that nobody really needed in the first place. Plus a ton more traffic right around our school, floods whenever it rains, and a thousand other problems."

"Well," said Beeks, "what do you expect us to do about it?"

I spoke up for the first time. "I think she expects us to, um, find a way to stop this."

Flynn said, "And how are we supposed to do *that*?"

Mrs. Starsky put her hand on Lizzie's shoulder and said, "Don't worry. I'm sure if we put our heads together, we can think of something."

After the meeting, Lizzie and I told Dodger about the FOR SALE sign. I figured he'd be upset, but he actually started out pretty calm. "Cool," he said. "What's a FOR SALE sign?"

"What do you mean, cool?" Lizzie shot back. "This isn't cool, it's a nightmare! A FOR SALE sign means somebody's trying to sell—" She gestured angrily toward my bedroom window, which looked over our backyard and into the woods. "Listen, Dodger, do you see that?" she shouted.

"Um, you mean the window? Why would any-body want to buy Willie's window?"

"Not the window—the view!"

"Whoa, dude, I didn't know you could even sell a view. But if they sell Willie's view, what are we go-ing to see when we look out the window?"

"They're not selling the view, Dodger. They're

25

selling the land. They're selling the forest. They're selling the Field of Dreams!"

Suddenly Dodger's unpatched eye bulged. "Ooooohh," he said, "I get it! Like when I helped those dudes with the bows and arrows sell Manhattan to the Dutch settlers. How dumb were those Dutch guys, anyway? We got 'em to give us, like, twenty-four bucks' worth of shells and beads for it—and then they realized they couldn't even carry the land away. Duh, like it was going to fit in their dinky little ships!"

Lizzie sat down on the bed and sighed. "Dodger, when people buy land, they don't think they can move it somewhere—they just want to build on it. You know, like now Manhattan is all covered with huge, tall buildings?"

"Oh. Oooohhhh," Dodger said. He sat down next to Lizzie. "So, did I get my buddies a good deal with the beads-and-shells thing?"

She patted him on the shoulder. "Not particularly, I'm afraid."

"Are you sure? Those were some seriously cool beads."

"I'm sure, Dodger. So that's why we can't let anybody buy our woods. Because would you rather have the Field of Dreams or a bunch of skyscrapers?"

"Um, Lizzie," I said, "how are we supposed to stop a bunch of grown-ups from buying and selling a piece of land? Plus, how is this *my* quest if it's your idea in the first place?"

Just then, my little sister, Amy, came barging in. Fortunately, she couldn't see Dodger, because only Lizzie and I could—but she suspected Lizzie and I had some kind of secret, so she was constantly snooping around in our business. "Hi, Lizzie," she said as she flung herself into my desk chair. "Hey, what piece of land? What quest? What's going on? Are you guys having a big adventure? Huh? Huh?"

"No big adventure, Amy. Just the same old boring stuff. We're doing some research for student council."

" 'Bout what? I can help. I'm a great researcher!"

Lizzie said, "We're trying to learn how to be environmental activists."

"We are?" I blurted.

Lizzie elbowed me in the ribs. It hurt. "Oh, Willie, you're so funny. Isn't he, Amy? Of course we are."

Amy said, "Well, why don't you just read Dad's book?"

"Um, which book?" I asked. Dad has written a lot of books, and truthfully, most of them are about pretty boring topics.

"You're kidding, right? I'm talking about *Save the Planet in Ten Easy Steps*. It's only, like, the most important environmentalist book of the last fifty years."

"How do *you* know?" I asked.

"Some guy named Kirkus Reviews said so. It's right on the back cover of the book."

"*Kirkus Reviews* isn't a person, Amy—it's a magazine. Dad once told me that only, like, five people even read it, though."

"Well, whatever. They think Dad is a genius. I have a copy of the book in my room, if you want to see for yourself."

"I have a copy, too, but—" I started to say.

Lizzie cut me off. "All right, Amy," she said. "Thank you very much."

Amy grinned at me. "See, Willie? You might think I'm annoying, but at least your girlfriend appreciates me."

Lizzie spluttered, "I'm not his . . . he's not . . . we're not . . . we're just friends."

Amy winked at us, then went to get Dad's book.

28

CHAPTER FOUR

Into the Woods

I HATE TO SAY IT, but Dad's book was actually helpful. It was organized into sections, and each section was full of strategies for defending the environment. The first section was called Pick Your Battle. I think we had already done that part. The second section, Find Your Hook, looked more promising. Lizzie skimmed it and told me the first thing we had to do was come up with something unique about the woods—something that would be lost forever if they got bulldozed. Dodger jumped up from where he had been dozing on the bed and said, "Excellent! A safari! Let's go!"

"Right now?" I said. "I haven't even done my

homework yet, and soon it's going to be dinner-time. Plus, I promised Mom I'd take out the garbage before—"

Lizzie rolled her eyes. "This is important, Willie," she said.

"It's an adventure!" Amy shouted as she charged into my room again.

"You're not going!" I yelled back.

"Oh, okay," Amy said. "I didn't realize this was, like, a date." Then she giggled her way back to her own room.

The next thing I knew, Lizzie and I were walking through the woods. I asked her what we were looking for, and all she told me was that I would know it when I saw it. Meanwhile, Dodger had magically changed into a whole safari outfit, complete with one of those baggy beige vests with a million pockets, matching shorts, and a big round hat. He had a butterfly net strapped to his back and a magnifying glass in one hand. Since I had no idea what I was even looking for, I spent a minute watching Dodger in action. He was stalking from tree to tree, studying the ground intently with every step. Every few seconds, he would bend over and use the magnifying glass to look at something up close before continuing on his way. Occasionally, he scratched his chin and said, "Hmmm" or "A-ha!"

Then, all of a sudden, he reached down, picked up a little stick, and said, "Behold!"

Lizzie came running over. "What is it, Dodger?"

He looked all excited. "Look!" he exclaimed. "It's the rare and elusive Four-Pronged Brown Twig!"

"Huh?" Lizzie and I both said at the same time.

"Check it out! Have you ever seen one of these before? I mean, sure, you can find Three-Pronged Brown Twigs all over the world. And the Five-Pronged Greenish Twig is fairly common. But a Four-Pronged Brown Twig? This has to be an endangered species or something."

He handed me the magnifying glass, and I leaned in for a better look while Lizzie got down on her hands and knees to investigate something on the forest floor. For a moment, I started feeling excited, too. It did look like a pretty interesting twig. But then Lizzie said, "Umm, Dodger, no offense, but here's another brown twig with four prongs. And here's another. I don't think your specimen is rare at all. Besides, twigs aren't even a species."

Dodger wandered off, disappointed. But then a moment later, he shouted, "It's a miracle! Call the newspapers! This bush looks exactly like Mount Rushmore!" It kind of did, if you tilted your head and squinted, but Lizzie said that wouldn't do the trick, either.

I walked away from Dodger and Lizzie, and tried to find something unique that would save our woods. I found some crushed-up soda cans, a few plastic bags, and a dead, smelly rat, but no rare plants or animals, as far as I could tell. I was about to turn around and give up when I saw a flash of green from behind a tree. I wasn't sure what I had seen, so I tiptoed over and peeked around the trunk, but whatever I had glimpsed was gone.

At that point, I did turn around and start walking back. But then I saw something green dashing through the underbrush again. I tried to sneak up on whatever it was, but of course I stepped on a stick. It made a loud cracking noise, and that was that. I swear, I have to be the lamest sneaker-upper in the history of the world.

When I got back to my friends, they were arguing. "There! Did you see it that time?" Lizzie asked.

"What are you talking about?" Dodger said. "I didn't see a thing. I don't know, maybe it's this stupid eye patch. I bet without it I'd be an excellent thing-seer. Why, we chimps are renowned far and wide for our strong scouting and investigating skills. For example, you might remember how that great explorer and adventurer Peter Panzee flew all the way from London to Never Never Land without even a compass. Or how my ancestors sailed the seven seas."

"They did?"

"Sure. Haven't you ever heard of Chimps Ahoy? Anyway, I didn't see any green flash in the trees. Especially not one with pointy ears!"

"Wait a minute," Lizzie said. "I never said anything about pointy ears! How did you—"

"Oooh, look at the time, kids! Looks like we'd better be getting back to your house before—"

"Wait a minute, Dodger!" I said. "I just saw something green sneaking around over behind that row of bushes, too. We can't leave now. What if it's some kind of new animal nobody's ever seen before? This could totally save the forest!"

"Nah, it was probably just a Minty Barksucker. Those aren't unusual at all."

"What the heck is a Minty Barksucker? Sounds rare to me!"

"Um, did I say Minty Barksucker? I meant to say

Green-Bellied Forest Eel. Very common, but extremely dangerous. Probably people see 'em all the time, but then the eels eat the people. That would explain if you haven't heard of them. Anyway, we'd better go before the eel notices us. Dude, I don't want to scare anybody or anything, but trust me—you don't want to meet up with a Green-Bellied Forest Eel. Let's just back away slowly. And, um, neither one of you has any cuts or scabs, right? Because the Green-Bellied Forest Eel tends to get enraged by the smell of blood. Or small fish. Are either of you carrying any anchovies?"

Lizzie and I shook our heads.

"Or sardines?"

We both shook our heads again.

"Mackerel?"

Lizzie stomped her foot. She said, "Dodger, there's no such thing as a Green-Bellied Forest Eel. That is the craziest thing I have ever heard! You're just making stuff up to get us to leave."

Dodger looked down at his feet. "Fine," he said. "You're right. But come on—wouldn't it be cool if there *were* Green-Bellied Forest Eels? Because, for one thing, then the Broad-Nosed Land Sharks wouldn't be so lonely. . . ."

Lizzie said, "Enough, Dodger! I want to find that pointy-eared creature that was sneaking around behind those trees. Now, would you come *on* already?"

Dodger made a pouty face and said, "Okay, if you insist. But it's probably just a leprechaun."

"Oh, forget it!" Lizzie said. "If you aren't going to be serious, I quit!"

She turned on her heel and marched in the direction of my backyard. I followed her. We didn't find out that he *had* been serious about the leprechaun until it was too late.

CHAPTER FIVE

Kissy Face and the Secret Seller

As soon as Lizzie and I stepped through the back door of my house, Amy was all over us. "So," she said, "did you find a rare animal to save?"

"No," I said.

"Did you find a rare plant to save?"

"No," Lizzie said.

"Did you hold hands and skip romantically through the forest?"

"NO!" we both shouted. Lizzie fled to the kitchen to call her mom. Unfortunately, Amy stayed with me. She bent toward me and whispered, "Did Lizzie make the Kissy Face?"

"What are you *talking* about?" I hissed.

"Oh, I think you know," she said.

"I don't know! I swear, Amy, I have no idea whatsoever."

Amy rolled her eyes and said, "How is it even possible that you are three years older than me? The Kissy Face is when the girl turns to you, like *this*, gazes at you with love, like *this*, and then starts to lean closer and closer to you like . . ."

That's when Lizzie walked back in and said, "My mum is going to come get me in about fifteen—what are you DOING?"

I jumped away from my little maniac of a sister and said, "Nothing!" just as Amy said, "I was just showing Willie the Kissy Face—you know, in case you've been trying to use it on him and he hasn't even noticed."

Lizzie gave her a completely blank look and said, "What are you talking about?"

"That's what I said!" I said.

"That *is* what you said," Amy said.

"Stop saying what I said," I said.

"Why?" Amy said. "You said you said what you said, so why can't I say you said what you said you said?"

"Aaagh! You are so annoying! Now leave us alone so we can work."

"Work, huh? Is that what you kids are calling it these days?" She winked at us. I couldn't believe it—she actually *winked* at us.

"Yes, work! Now get going!"

Amy headed up to her room, but turned at the top of the stairs to blow kisses at us. I felt my face heating up in a massive blush. Unfortunately, I am a major blusher.

Lizzie turned to me and said, "Honestly, do you have any idea what that was all about?"

"Nope," I said.

"Are you sure? You haven't been—well—saying anything that would make your sister think we were—I mean—"

"NO!" I shouted.

Lizzie said, "Whew! Thank goodness, because that would be awkward. Can you even imagine you and me—"

"NO!" I said quickly.

"Me, either," Lizzie said. But for some strange reason, I could have sworn she was blushing a little bit, too.

We went into the family room and got to work. Lizzie started flipping through my dad's book. "What does it say to do if there's nothing rare about the land you're trying to save?" I asked.

"I dunno," Lizzie said. "Ooh, wait! The next chapter is called Follow the Money. Apparently, we need to find out who owns the woods, and who will make money if they get sold."

"How do we do that?" I asked.

"It says here there are three ways. We could call the real estate agent who's selling the property, we could go to Town Hall and do our research there, or we could check the Internet."

Bingo! I thought. *I am a whiz at finding stuff out on the Internet.* I sat down at our family computer and started searching for "WOODS" and "SALE." I got something like 50,000 results, and none of the ones I looked at had anything to do with our woods. I tried "FOREST" and "REAL ESTATE," and again I got a ton of random results. Lizzie told me to move over and smushed herself onto the chair with me, but she couldn't find anything, either.

Just then, Dodger came strolling in the back door. "Hi, dudes!" he said. "Have you seen my Bottomless

Well of Treats?" That's a magical bag that automatically fills itself with any food you wish for. "I'm, like, completely starving. I think I'll have some bananas. And then some grapes. Mmmm, grapes! And then maybe I'll wish for more bananas. And then a nice basket of apples. Or maybe oranges. I don't know which I like better, really—it's kind of like comparing apples and oranges. Ooh, so *that's* what that saying means!"

"Dodger," Lizzie said, "we're trying to get some work done here. Do you mind?"

"Nope, why would I mind? I mean, it's not like I ever ignore you just because I'm in the middle of some dumb old project when you're in the mood to play or anything."

"But you're always in the mood to play."

Dodger thought about that for a minute, then said, "That's kinda true. I think it's part of my charm, though. Anyway, wanna play Frisbee?"

Lizzie and I shook our heads.

"Checkers?"

We both shook our heads again.

"Fear-ball?" Fear-ball is this terrifying game Dodger had invented to make me better at baseball. Long story.

40

"No," Lizzie said. "This is really important work."

"Can I help?" Dodger asked, pulling another chair over near the computer.

"Well, I don't really think you'd be—"

"What, you think I'm not good at computers? Oh, sure—because I happen to be a chimpanzee, right? How do you know I'm not, like, a total computer genius? For all you know, I'm the greatest computer-chimp that ever lived. For all you know, I spend days, months, even years on the computer when I'm in my lamp. I might be a world-famous expert. I might get calls from all over the planet asking for my unique blend of technological know-how and general adorableness. Is that a word? Anyway, I might be all of those things—but you'll never know, because you never thought to ask if—"

"Hey, Dodger?" Lizzie asked. "Do you know anything about computers?"

Dodger leaned closer, examined the computer screen, looked at Lizzie, looked at me, and then reached down and pulled the computer's plug out of the wall. "Nope," he said. "Give me a break. I'm a chimp—why would I need to know anything about computers?"

41

Lizzie looked like she might reach out and smack Dodger on the head.

But then he spoke again. "On the other hand, I do know exactly who owns the woods. I mean, if you're interested."

The next day, after school, Lizzie and I took a walk downtown. On a little side alley I had never noticed before, we found a small storefront office that looked brand-new. In fact, the paint on the sign over the door was so shiny and wet-looking that we thought it would drip on our heads as we walked in. The fancy, old-fashioned lettering said:

Bottled Hope, Incorporated
T. G. Lasorda, President
Real Estate, Tax Advice, Miracles
CREDIT CARDS AND MAGICAL GOLD LUMPS ACCEPTED

Inside, we found ourselves facing a huge wooden desk with a familiar figure behind it. He was wearing a shiny suit made of what appeared to be gold threads, a blindingly white dress shirt, and a ruby-red tie, along with a matching red beret tilted atop his head. He had oily, jet-black hair and a pointy little goatee, which set off his coal-black eyes and evil little grin.

"Hello, kiddies!" said the Great Lasorda in a voice that sounded like he had just finished gargling a mouthful of honey. "What can I do for you on this fine day? Are you looking to buy a house? Hire a tax advisor? Make a few wishes?" It had only been about a month since I had last seen the Great Lasorda, but I had almost forgotten how much he irritated me. He is an ancient, powerful genie, and Dodger used to work for him—until I had wished for Dodger to be free.

I guess you could say old The Great and I don't see eye to eye.

I got right to the point. "You're selling the woods!"

He stuck his finger into the gap between his neck and the collar of his shirt and pulled at the fabric. "Oh, I do hate the way these French silks chafe me! I have such sensitive skin, and it's not like the old days, when I had an army of tailors to handcraft my wardrobe. Anyway, William—or should I say 'Willers'?—you are correct. I am selling that adorable little plot of land behind your house."

"Why?" Lizzie asked. "You know Dodger's Field of Dreams is in there! Plus, it's going to ruin the whole neighborhood!"

His Great Royal Magicness yawned, then slowly took out a nail file and began buffing his nails. "And?"

"And it doesn't make any sense!" I said. "Why would a genie need to sell anything, anyway?"

"Little boy, style *costs*. Do you think it's easy maintaining my legend? How long do most movie stars last, hmmm? I've been at the forefront of fashion for three thousand years, and I'm not about to lose that now."

"But . . . but . . ." I stammered, "couldn't you just make whatever you need? Or snap your fingers and make the money to pay for everything?"

Lasorda held his hand out in front of his face, blew on his fingernails, frowned, and started buffing again. "Well, I *could*," he said. "But it's a lot more complicated than that. There are tax consequences— the government *hates* it when you create money magically. Especially if you put your own face on the bills, apparently. But what was I supposed to do, leave that tacky Franklin fellow plastered all over everything?"

"So why don't you just—" Lizzie began.

"Oh, are *you* still here?" Lasorda said. "I don't need to tell either of you why I do anything. I am selling the forest, which *I* own, to raise some cash, which *I* need. Case closed. Class dismissed. Over and out. Ta-ta! Cheerio! *Hasta la vista!*"

He swiveled his chair so his back was to us and started filing the nails on his other hand. I looked at Lizzie, who gestured in Lasorda's direction and mouthed, *Do something, Willie!* I hate when people tell me to do something but don't tell me what I'm supposed to do. Don't they know I have no self-confidence?

I cleared my throat. "Uh, Your Magicness? Sir?"

Lasorda sounded even more annoyed with me than he had been, if that was possible. He sighed and said, "Yes, William?"

I thought fast. "How much are you selling the woods *for*?"

He spun back around and leaned toward us. "Why do you ask?"

I forced myself to take a slow, deep breath, and said, "Well, I might be able to find you a buyer. Or something."

And then the Great Lasorda laughed in my face. Boy, if there's anything I hate more than people telling me to *do something*, it's people laughing in my face. "Oh, William!" he said when he was done making a big show of chuckling until he couldn't breathe. "As if you could possibly know anyone who has enough gold to pay off the lepre—I mean, the people I need to pay. For some items I recently, ah, purchased."

When people laugh at me, I sometimes get a little stubborn. "Why?" I asked. "How much could you possibly owe to, um, whoever you're talking about?"

"Do you really want to know?"

I nodded.

"Do you really, *really* want to know?"

I nodded again.

"Do you really, really, *really* want to—"

Lizzie stomped her foot and said, "Would you just tell us already?"

The Great Lasorda got all huffy for a moment, but then the slick smile spread across his face again. "If you really, really, really want to know all the details, I'd suggest you go home and ask your little chimp friend. After all, this whole situation is his fault!"

CHAPTER SIX

How Was I Supposed to Know Magic Was so Expensive?

THE NEXT DAY AFTER SCHOOL, I decided Dodger and I needed to have a little talk. When I got home, I went right up to my room and knocked on his lamp. For a moment, nothing happened, but then he appeared in a POOF! of blue smoke. He was gasping for breath.

"Dude," he said, "I am so totally tired! I was playing this brutal new game on my Wii Fit in a Lamp system."

"What's it called?" I asked.

"Wii Wii Tennis."

"Don't you mean Wii Tennis?"

47

"No, that's easy. This is Wii Wii Tennis. You actually have to control the guy who's controlling the guy who's playing tennis. It's way, way harder. Not as hard as Wii Wii Wii Football, though. Once I slipped playing that, and the Arizona Cardinals wound up in the Super Bowl! Anyway, what's up? You look all stressed out. Life's too short, my friend. You should just try to relax and enjoy every minute. Take my day, for example: I spend some time playing games, then I chill a little and, um, play games. By then, it's totally lunchtime. So I play this game called Throw Each Bite up in the Air and Catch It Without—OOPS! By the time I get that all cleaned up, it's nap time. Then more games. Or—wait a minute, I forgot Banana Time. But after Banana Time, guess what I do?"

"Play more games?"

"Nope, another nap. See, if you double up on naps, it gives you that extra edge for your late afternoon playing."

"Okay, that's great advice, Dodger. Now can I ask you something?"

Dodger started jumping down. "Yes, I *will* play Fear-ball: Winter Edition with you! Thanks for asking!"

Oh, jeepers. Fear-ball is this game Dodger invented to stop me from being afraid of catching a baseball. Basically, it consists of Dodger throwing balls at me really hard while I stand perfectly still. He's supposed to miss on purpose, but the first time we played it, he had nailed me in the head with a football so hard that I'd had a mark on my forehead for days. I had no idea what the Winter Edition part meant, but it didn't seem likely that asking for an explanation would help.

So that's how I ended up in the woods with Dodger. I was all bundled up in my winter coat, hat, gloves, scarf, boots, and even an embarrassing, poofy ski hat with orange tassels that my mom had once bought me—it wasn't particularly cold out, but I figured the more cushioning I had on, the better. Dodger was wearing plain blue shorts, a blue eye patch, and a pair of blue flip-flops.

Dodger led me straight to the Field of Dreams, which was somehow magically covered with dazzling, blue snow. He galloped into the clearing, and I suddenly realized I was in trouble. Wearing all blue, against a blue background, Dodger was nearly invisible. I tried to keep my eyes on his retreating back, but the next thing I knew, I couldn't find him at all.

"Hey, where'd you go?" I shouted. "And what am I supposed to—oof!"

A note to the reader: Getting hit in the stomach by a blue snowball is exactly as painful as getting hit in the stomach by a white one. Plus, you can't see a blue snowball coming at you if it's being thrown by a blue hand in a blue field. And chimps have really, really strong throwing arms.

I scrambled behind a tree just as a second snowball thwacked into a branch over my head. What was I going to do? How was I going to get through this game without getting totally pounded?

Answer: I wasn't. So I might as well ask Dodger my questions while he was pelting me. "Hey, Dodger," I shouted. "Why is the Great Lasorda selling these woods?"

Another snowball whizzed past my ear, and I realized Dodger was circling around so that the tree wasn't between us anymore. I backed slowly around the trunk as Dodger said, "Ah, trying to get me to talk, are you? Yeah, like that's going to work. You can't fool me, mister! I see right through your tricks."

Holy-moley. I hadn't meant this as a trick, but hey—it appeared to be working for me. Quickly, I bent down and packed a pretty big snowball.

"What did you think, dude—that I was just going to keep talking and talking until you hit me with a snowball? I mean, it's not like I'm some kind of blabbermouth. Why, back in Chimptopia, I was widely admired for my strong, silent personality and excellent discipline. Haven't I ever told you about the time I sat in a banana tree for seventeen straight days without—oof!"

I dusted my hands off, ran behind a different tree, and started making another snowball. *Score one for the little guy*, I thought. The battle was on. "So," I yelled, "I guess I can't get you to tell me about this Lasorda thing, huh? Since you're too clever to be fooled . . ."

"That's right. I know some chimps might get all distracted and start telling you how Lasorda spent way too much gold on the magic potions I asked for. But not me! I'm way too smart for that. Plus, I am quite stealthy. I move like the night! I am the Ninja of the Jungle! I can't be seen, heard, or even—HAH! Missed me! Anyway, you won't get a peep out of me!"

I stepped out from behind a rock to face the sound of Dodger's voice. "Wait a minute! What gold? What magic potions?"

Of course, he totally pegged me with a snowball, knocking me on my butt and giving me a massive nosebleed. The last thing I heard before I passed out was footsteps bounding toward me and Dodger shouting, "I win! I win! I—ooh, that doesn't look good! Hey, Willie, guess what? Did you know blood makes blue snow look purple?"

I woke up flat on my back in the field, but all the snow was gone. Except for one last ball that Dodger had stuffed inside my hat to make an ice pack. He was holding the ice pack to the side of my nose with one hand, and arguing on a blue cell phone that he was holding in the other one.

I tried really hard not to gag on the mixture of blood and melting snow that was flowing down into my mouth. Dodger was having a *very* interesting conversation, and I didn't want him to find out I was awake and stop talking. I could only hear his side of the discussion, with pauses in between, but it sounded like he was getting first aid tips—and talking about why Lasorda was selling the forest.

"Yes, I'm pressing the ice pack against his nose. Now what? Oh, he's just going to wake up? Are you sure? Really? Dude, these humans sure are fragile!"

Then there was a pause as Dodger readjusted

the ice pack. Suddenly I felt a push on my nose as Dodger responded to whatever he was hearing on the phone. It hurt.

"Wait, I can't tell him that!" Dodger yelled into the phone. "He'll think it's, like, all his fault that the woods are being sold!"

"Well, we needed the disguise potion so I could go to school and be Willie!"

"YES, we needed the Tincture of Distraction, too. And the Essence of Belief. And the magic dust. So Willie could get elected president, of course!"

"And of *course* I knew the leprechauns would want to be paid. But the Great Lasorda didn't tell me he didn't have the gold to pay for them."

"He said that?"

"He said *that*?"

"He said *THAT*? Dude, I swear, I had no idea. Man, Willie is going to be so sad if the Great Lasorda sells the woods. Maybe if I just go back to work for Lasorda, he might forget this whole thing. Or maybe he could, like, lend me to the leprechauns for a while. I mean, how long could it possibly take to work off a hundred thousand golden coins?"

Oh, no, I thought. Dodger had worked for the Great Lasorda for thousands of years, until I had used a magical wish to ask for Dodger's freedom. I didn't want him to have to go back after all we had been through together. I sat up so suddenly that Dodger yanked his hand away from my nose and yelped. "Dodger," I said, "you can't go back to Lasorda. You just can't!"

"But what about the forest? What about your big quest? We can't just let the trees get chopped down and everything."

"We'll think of something. We always think of something. Right?"

Dodger gave me a crushing hug. Which made my nose start bleeding again. Meanwhile, Dodger's phone fell on the frozen ground, and I could hear a faint voice coming from it: *Dodger, are you still there, present, accounted for?*

"Dodger," I said, "why didn't you just tell me all this stuff? Why would Rodger know everything if *I* didn't?" Rodger is Dodger's brother, who still works for Lasorda. Rodger and Dodger look almost exactly alike, but you can tell who's who when they speak. Rodger has a strange habit of talking in synonyms.

"Uh, can I call you back?" Dodger asked.

Sure, fine, A-OK, no problemo, Rodger said.

Then Dodger hung up and looked at me. "Buddy," he said, "I think I messed up."

Then he explained everything to me. I had always thought Lasorda just made all of the magical potions Dodger had used in our adventures together, but apparently Lasorda had been buying them from a group of leprechauns that live in our forest. Dodger had been promising all along that he would pay Lasorda back, and now the leprechauns had started asking Lasorda for the gold.

Jeepers. This was a pretty complicated situation. "A hundred thousand gold pieces, huh?" I asked.

"Yeah," Dodger replied. "Is that a lot?"

I sighed and patted him on the shoulder. My head hurt. "Let's go home, okay?" I said. Then we trudged off through the woods, leaving a purple patch of blood in the blue snow.

CHAPTER SEVEN

Sold!

"DOES IT HURT A LOT?" Lizzie asked me at lunch the next day.

My nose had swollen up overnight, and people had been asking about it all morning. At home, I had made up an elaborate excuse about a branch falling off a tree and hitting me, but at school I was just telling everyone I had "run into something." Unfortunately, I had a feeling my parents and sister hadn't believed the excuse about the branch—and the last thing I needed was to give Amy a reason to snoop around even more than usual.

"Only when I breathe," I said.

"Ha-ha. So, Willie, what are we going to tell the

student council today? Do we have a plan for saving the forest or not?"

"Not exactly," I said. "Why don't we tell them we're working on it? That's what mayors and governors always say when they don't have a good answer."

"All right. But we will have to find something useful to do really soon. Otherwise, Dodger and everything else that lives in the forest will be in real trouble."

Everything else that lives in the forest? I thought. *Hmmm* . . . Maybe I would be able to come up with a plan after all. I just needed a little more time to think.

After school, at student council, Lizzie told the group that she and I had been doing research in order to save the forest. Some of the younger kids looked kind of impressed, but one third grader said, "Research? Isn't that, like, reading? How is reading stuff going to help a forest?"

"Research isn't just reading," I said. "Sometimes you have to do science experiments, or go searching for information on the computer."

"And sometimes you even have to find information out in the world," Lizzie added.

"Like what?" Beeks said.

"Like the name of the person who's selling the land," Lizzie fired back.

"So, how does that matter?" Craig Flynn asked.

"Well, maybe we could convince the person not to sell the property," Lizzie said.

"Or maybe we could find someone to buy the woods who would promise not to knock them down," I added.

"Oh, really?" Beeks said. "Who in the world would want to do that? What good are a bunch of stupid old trees, anyway? It's not like the trees *do* anything."

Mrs. Starsky put her hand on Beeks's shoulder and said, "A forest is more than a bunch of trees, James. It's also a factory for making the oxygen we all breathe. Plus, it's a home for thousands and thousands of different plants and animals."

"Oh, and that's another thing," I said. "If we could find some kind of rare living thing in the forest, maybe we could convince the town that the woods have to be saved."

"Good thinking, Willie," Mrs. Starsky said.

Good thinking, Willie, I could see Beeks mouthing with a smirk behind her back.

"Have you actually tried to find anything in there?" a fourth-grade girl asked.

"We went exploring in the woods yesterday, but we didn't find anything that looked particularly rare," Lizzie admitted.

"What if you had help?" a kindergartner asked. "My mom says I'm excellent at finding stuff. I mean, during the vacation, I found every single one of my Hanukkah presents. They were in my dad's closet, behind his sneakers. That was a pretty good hiding place, because nobody wants to touch Dad's sneakers, believe me. So anyway, I think I would be an excellent strange-creature hunter."

All of the other little kids liked that. Instantly, we had a ton of volunteers to help us comb the forest for odd wildlife. Then Lizzie decided to sign kids up for other tasks, like writing letters to the town council and the newspapers, researching the history of the forest, and reading up on endangered local species. It was pretty cool. In about five minutes, we went from having to do everything all by ourselves to having our own workforce. In fact, the sign-ups went so well that soon there were only two people who hadn't volunteered: James Beeks and Craig Flynn.

Lizzie went to work. "You know, James," she said, "what we need now is someone who could be in charge of working with the town government on this. You'd be great for that job, with all of your political experience and all. Plus, I think you could really impress a lot of people by saving the forest. You'd be showing everyone what a true leader you are."

"Oh, yeah? Like who?"

"Like . . . I don't know . . . your dad?" Ooh, that was a good one. We knew from experience that James had a major issue with trying to impress his father.

"My dad has more important things to worry about than a bunch of trees."

"Yes, but he would definitely be happy to see you taking charge of a major political operation . . . working with the town council and the mayor . . . getting big things done. Unless you'd rather have me give the job to someone else. I'd imagine there are plenty of fourth graders who could use this when they run for student council president next year."

Beeks whispered a few words to Craig Flynn, who whispered back. They seemed to be arguing for a minute or so, but then they both nodded. "Fine,"

James said. "We'll do it. I'll write the letters and make the phone calls, and Craig here can, um, bake cookies for the next town council meeting."

"Bake *cookies*?" Craig growled. "I'm too tough to bake cookies."

"You know," Lizzie said, "whoever bakes the cookies gets to eat as many as he wants when they're done."

"Oh, fine," Craig said. "But don't expect me to wear an apron or anything."

Beeks smirked at him. "Nah. But maybe one of those cool white hats with the poofy part on top?"

And that was that. It looked like we had the student council on board in our fight to save the woods. I told all of the kids who were doing research that they should come to our next meeting with information, and then I adjourned the meeting. That means I got to bang the gavel again, which wasn't as much fun as usual because the vibration running up my arm made my nose hurt.

Lizzie and I spent the week between meetings reading up on endangered and threatened animals in our state, hanging out with Dodger, and trying to keep Amy from driving us totally nuts. She followed us everywhere with lists of animals, names of wildlife protection organizations, and of course her trusty Sherlock Holmes tools. If you've never been stalked by a second grader who carries a magnifying glass and wears a checkered hat with earflaps, you just don't know what you're missing.

And you probably want to keep it that way.

Because Amy was around all the time, Dodger had to lay low. From what I could tell, he spent a lot of time in his lamp. From the occasional snippets of the Chimptopian national anthem that floated from the lamp at odd hours, I got the feeling he was also on the phone a lot. I hoped he was arguing with the Great Lasorda. I mean, I knew Lasorda was annoying and pushy, but I hadn't thought he was the kind of guy who would sell the whole forest for so little reason.

Unless Lasorda was trying to threaten Dodger into going back to work for him. Or maybe he wanted to sell the forest so he could pay the leprechauns back, but take away their homes at the same time. That would be really, really sneaky. Jeepers. As soon as money is involved, life gets really complicated.

The day of the next meeting rolled around, and Lizzie and I decided to meet early before school to make one last check for forest creatures. Amy had told us that sometimes different species are visible at different times of day, and all of our other exploration visits had been in the afternoons. Lizzie had a list of animals to look for, along with a picture of each. There was a tiny mammal called the Least Shrew that looked kind of like a mouse with a long, pointy nose, a reptile called the Bog Turtle, and an amphibian called the Spotted Salamander. There was even something called a Flying Squirrel, which sounded kind of alarming. I didn't mention it to Lizzie, but I had a feeling I might have to run away and hide if I saw one of those coming at me.

We were just about to step off the sidewalk and into the forest when Amy came bounding around the corner. "Can I go with you guys? Huh? Huh? I promise I won't bother you at all. I'll just help you look. I mean, six eyes are better than four, right? Unless your strangely invisible companion is meeting you here, too, in which case eight eyes are better than six."

The worst thing about Amy's constant snooping is how smart she is. Even though she couldn't see Dodger, she somehow seemed to know that Lizzie and I had an unseen friend. Once she had even asked us whether we were hanging out with a blue orangutan, and I denied it. Which wasn't exactly lying, since Dodger is a chimpanzee. But anyway, we couldn't possibly bring her into the woods with us. What if she somehow found the Field of Dreams? Or spotted a leprechaun? Or kept up her nonstop talking and drove every animal in the forest into hiding?

"Amy, please go home," I said. I really didn't want to be mean, but there was just no way I was taking her in there.

"No," she said. "We're already halfway to school, and I don't want to go home and take the bus. Plus, you need me."

"Yeah, right," I said.

"You totally do. Watch, I'll ask you some questions to prove it. Where in the forest would you look for a Least Shrew?"

"Ummm . . ."

"See, told ya. And where would you find a Bog Turtle?"

"Uh, in a bog?"

"And what, exactly, is a bog?"

"I don't know. Maybe we'll just look for the turtle, and wherever we find it, that's a bog."

"All right, I just have one more question: Who bought the forest?"

"What are you talking about?" Lizzie and I both asked at once.

"I'm talking about *that*!" Amy exclaimed. She was pointing to the FOR SALE sign at the edge of the sidewalk. Someone had stapled a big red banner to the bottom, with just one word on it:

SOLD!

CHAPTER EIGHT

Beeks, Beeks, Beeks, and Son

ONCE WE FOUND OUT the disastrous news that the forest had already been sold, Lizzie and I didn't even bother going in to look for rare animals. We just walked the rest of the way to school, with Amy trailing behind.

"I wonder who bought the woods," Amy said. "Maybe it's a huge real estate developer and they're going to put a hundred outlet stores in there. That would be the worst—wall-to-wall pavement as far as the eye can see. And can you imagine the view from our windows at home? Parking lots—yuck! Or maybe a garbage company is going to put a massive dump there. And they're going to throw disgusting stuff in: Dead bodies! Bloody pig guts from butcher stores! Toxic chemicals! Yikes! We'd never be able to open our windows again! On the other hand, maybe a hospital is going to build a psycho ward. And they're going to send all the craziest madmen in the state to live there! All day long, we'll hear their disturbed laughter. And then at night, we'll be awakened by the terrifying screams of their tormented—"

I couldn't take listening anymore, so I snapped, "Could you just be quiet for a change, Amy? You are NOT helping! Why can't you just leave us alone?"

Amy looked at me like I had just thrown something at her. For a moment, I thought she was going to cry, but then she just stomped away from us and into the school yard. Lizzie turned to me and said, "Why did you do that, Willie? She's not that bad. And she really *does* try to help."

I sighed. "I know you're right. It's just that she never stops. I'll tell her I'm sorry later, okay?"

Lizzie nodded and we went into school.

At the student council meeting, a lot of the younger kids were very excited to show us all the work they had done to learn more about the forest. It was pretty interesting. Kids had drawn life-size pictures of several animals (as it turns out, bog turtles are kind of cute); made maps, charts, and graphs (it was sad to see how little wild land was left in our area and how fast it was disappearing); and even brought in little dioramas of animal habitats (it's amazing how many animals can live in a forest if nobody cuts the trees down). The excitement was running so high that I couldn't even bear to tell them the bad news about the SOLD banner.

As soon as I banged the gavel, I gave all of the council members time to show us what they had learned. Then, because I knew I had to tell them sooner or later, I told the group that the land had already been sold. That got everybody really riled up, and kids started shouting out ideas for what to do next:

"Let's call the mayor!"

"No, let's call the governor!"

"No, let's call the newspaper!"

"Hey, why don't we form a human chain and block the bulldozers?"

"What bulldozers?"

"You know, the ones that are going to knock down the forest."

"Oh, *those* bulldozers."

"Hey, I think bulldozers are cool! I saw this one show where a bulldozer totally flattened a hill in about five seconds flat. And then they put a car in front of it, and the bulldozer turned the car into a twisted pile of smoking wreckage. It was awesome!"

"Uh, can we focus for a minute here?" Lizzie said. "We really do have to act fast now. We will still need to gather evidence to prove that building on our woods would be a bad idea. Then we're going to need to get the word out to the government, the newspapers and TV stations, and everybody in town. We'll need committees, volunteers, sign-up sheets! We're not going to take this lying down!"

Then James Beeks said, "You might as well forget it, Lizzie. I mean, it's not like the town council is going to listen to a bunch of little kids, anyway."

"What are you talking about, James? We're just getting started."

"Yeah, but doesn't it seem kind of pointless?

Whatever they're going to build there, they're going to have to build it somewhere. So even if you do stop them from knocking down these woods, you're not really saving the planet, anyway."

Wow, that sounded kind of logical. I hate it when Beeks starts sounding reasonable.

"James," Lizzie said, "what's going on? At the last meeting, you agreed to help."

"I know, but . . . look, maybe we should just have a big bake sale to raise money for charity. We'd be doing something totally useful, and . . . and . . . and Craig would even wear an apron!"

Craig jumped up. "What? Why would I have to wear the apron? Why couldn't you wear it? Why do I always have to do the dirty work, huh?"

James looked down for a minute, then back up at Lizzie. I couldn't believe it: He almost looked like he was apologizing for something. "Lizzie, please. I'll even wear the apron. I'll wear ten aprons—pink ones. With bunnies on 'em. Just don't make us do this forest thing."

Lizzie was speechless. So was everybody else, until Mrs. Starsky broke the silence. "All right, kids. Time's up for today. Let's all take a few days to see what happens, okay? In the meantime, Willie and

Lizzie can work on finding out who is supposed to buy the land. Then maybe we can vote on our next steps when we meet again."

I was so confused I almost pounded the gavel down on my own hand. Why had James suddenly tried to get us to change our project? He had been negative at first, but that was different; it was just his usual sniping at anything Lizzie or I said. Now he was almost begging us to do something else. And was he right? Was saving the forest a hopeless idea?

My head hurt.

Lizzie had a dentist appointment after the meeting, and Amy had left when school got out, so I walked home all alone. As I drew within sight of the spot on the sidewalk where the FOR SALE sign had been, I couldn't help noticing it looked different somehow. For a few moments, I felt hopeful. Maybe the project had been canceled! Maybe we had just imagined the SOLD banner! Yeah, right. And maybe my ninety-year-old aunt Ida is going to run away and join the Marines.

When I got close enough to see, the sign was different. In fact, the old sign was completely gone, and in its place was a larger one:

COMING SOON:
WOODLAND ACRES FUNPLEX
FOOD! RIDES! GAMES!
BASEBALL BATTING CAGES!
ANOTHER FINE PROJECT BROUGHT TO YOUR
COMMUNITY BY
BEEKS, BEEKS, BEEKS, AND SON, INC.

This was terrible! I ran the rest of the way home and tried to call Lizzie, but then I remembered she was at the dentist. I was dying to tell somebody about all this, but my mom was working late, my dad was locked in his office, writing, and Amy—well, you can see why I didn't want to go blabbing to Amy. I charged up to my room and rubbed the side of Dodger's lamp. He didn't come out right away, so in my excitement, I might have knocked on it—a little too hard.

Dodger appeared next to me in his usual POOF! of blue smoke. He was swaying from side to side, holding his head. As soon as his eyes focused on me, he said, "Earthquake! Willie, we have to get out of here before the whole house—oh, wait. Why aren't we shaking? That was a pretty short earthquake."

Oops. "Um, it wasn't an earthquake. You just didn't come out when I rubbed, so I started knocking. I guess I got a little carried away."

"Ah, it's no big deal. I didn't really like those ancient Greek statues on my table, anyway."

Double oops.

"So what's the emergency, dude? Is Lizzie in trouble? Is Amy hurt? Did I miss a meal?"

"No, it's just bad news about the forest. I was walking home and—"

Just then, Amy started pounding on my door. I jumped about three feet. Dodger whispered, "Whoa, bud. What's with your family and banging on stuff today?"

Amy shouted, "Willie, who's shouting in there? I just saw you go into your room by yourself a minute ago, and now I hear somebody screaming."

"Uh, it's just a computer game," I said.

"Oh, yeah? What's it called, *My Brother Is a Big, Fat Liar: The Game*?"

I knew I had been a little mean to her that morning, but this was too much. I shouted back, "For the last time, Amy, LEAVE ME ALONE! What I do is none of your business!"

She said, "You know, I just want to know what's going on with you and your friends."

Then it just slipped out. I was mad at James Beeks, mad at the world, and annoyed with Amy, so I yelled, "Well, maybe if you got some friends of your own, you wouldn't have to worry about mine all the time!"

I heard Amy's footsteps running away down the hall, and then her door slamming shut with a bang. Meanwhile, Dodger was staring at me. I waited for him to tell me to apologize, or something. But all he said was, "Dude." Then he sighed and said, "Let's get out of here. I've been stuck in my lamp all day, and you're going, like, bonkers."

I wasn't really in the mood for fun, but it was better than sitting around feeling guilty about my sister. "What do you want to do?" I asked.

"You'll see. Meet me at the field, pronto!" With that, he disappeared. I walked out of my room, walked down the hall trying not to look at Amy's closed door, went downstairs, left a note for my parents, and headed for the Field of Dreams. As I walked down the path from my backyard, I told myself I should try to enjoy the rest of the afternoon. After all, who knew how many more times we'd get to play there?

Just before the trees closed in around me, I took a look back at my house. For a split second, I saw Amy's sad face in the window. I almost waved, but before I could even get my hand up, her curtains swooshed shut and she was out of sight.

CHAPTER NINE

One Last Game?

DODGER WAS WAITING FOR ME at the Field of Dreams. He was all suited up to play baseball, even though it was the middle of winter and there were patches of slush and ice all over the diamond. His jersey said Pittsburgh Primates. He threw one at me that said Philadelphia Willies. It seemed like a nutty idea to drop everything and play ball in this situation, but I didn't bother to ask Dodger to explain. I generally find that asking Dodger questions just makes things more confusing.

I went behind the backstop to put on my jersey, and when I came back out, Rodger was there, too, sporting a hoodie that said World Chimpions on the front. He was standing on the pitcher's mound, clearing snow off the rubber with one foot. He had a glove on one hand and was tossing a baseball up and catching it again and again in the other. "Ah, spring!" Rodger exclaimed.

"Um, it's not spring yet," I said. "Technically, winter only just started a few weeks ago."

Rodger frowned at me, then continued. "Yes, spring! The scent, the odor, the perfume of the flowers wafting through the pollen-filled air. The evening sun, that magnificent golden eye, casting its warm rays on the grassy field of play."

Actually, it was getting dark pretty rapidly, although somehow it never really gets too dark to see on our field. But it would take more than a total mismatch with reality to stop Rodger when he's on a roll. "And the ball, ready to fly from pitcher's hand to catcher's outstretched mitt, unless by some stroke of chance the batter connects, makes contact, drives the ball into the vasty depths of the fresh-mowed outfield. Yes, it is time: time to test the might of my good right arm against the pluck, the determination, the sheer courage of the young man in the batter's box."

Dodger came over and put an arm around me.

"I think what my bro is trying to say is, PLAY BALL!" He crouched down behind home plate, held out a huge, old-fashioned catcher's glove in front of him, and gestured toward a bat that was leaning against the backstop. It was an awesome bat, made of some mysterious jet-black material, with my name written near the sweet spot in sparkling red letters. I picked up the bat and took a few practice swings. Of course, the bat felt perfect in my hands. I stepped into the batter's box and took a deep breath. Oddly, I almost thought I *could* smell a little whiff of fresh-cut grass.

What was I going to do without this place?

As Rodger went into his windup, I stepped away from the plate. "Dodger," I said, "we have a really huge problem."

Rodger delivered a perfect strike right down the middle of the plate and into Dodger's glove. "You're right," Rodger shouted. "The problem is that you can't hit my fastball, my heater, the high cheese."

If you've ever wondered whether being taunted by a chimpanzee is a good cure for a bad mood, here's your answer: It isn't. "Guys, I'm serious. The field is being sold."

"Dude, we knew that," Dodger said as he tossed the ball back to Rodger.

"Yeah, we knew Lasorda was trying to sell it. But now he has a buyer. Do you know what this means?"

Rodger threw a screaming fastball that hit Dodger's mitt with a loud thwap. "Uh, strike two?" Dodger said. He tossed the ball back to his brother.

"No, it means all of this is really going to be gone forever if we don't do something."

Rodger said, "But you ARE doing something. You're acting! You're fighting back!" He wound up and blew the ball by me again. "You're striking out!"

"Ha-ha." I put the bat down. "And guess who the buyer is? James Beeks's dad! He's *James Beeks's dad*! Do you know what that means?"

"His last name is Beeks, too?" Dodger said.

"Very funny. It means that Beeks went home and told his dad to buy the forest. James was supposed to be helping the student council save this place, and instead he betrayed us in a second as soon as he got the chance. Like he wasn't enough of a jerk already, now he goes and does this!"

Rodger threw a slow, slow pitch past me and yelled, "Second batter! Strike one! Boy, all this anger is having a bad, counterproductive, negative effect on your hitting."

That was it. Now I was even madder. Rodger got ready to pitch again and I got into my batting stance for the first time since baseball season had ended. He delivered, and I smacked the ball into a snowbank all the way out by the left-field fence.

"Whoa!" Dodger said. "Willie, that was awesome!" Truthfully, even though I was so mad, hitting the ball that far on my very first swing of the season really did feel great. I decided to do what Rodger and Dodger both wanted me to do, which was stop talking and start playing. They let me bat for a while more, and then Rodger pitched to Dodger and let me field—not that there was much fielding for me to do. I had never seen Dodger hit before, but holy cow! He hit pitch after pitch out of the park. Dodger had once hinted that he had taught Babe Ruth to hit home runs, and for the first time, I sort of believed him. He had a short, abrupt swing, but I guess magical chimps are just super strong, because the balls jumped off his bat. After every big hit, he shouted, "Du-u-ude!" at the top of his lungs and laughed with joy. By the third or fourth homer, I was laughing with him.

Eventually, Rodger ended the practice by claiming that his arm was getting, and I quote, "sore, weary, fatigued."

Then the three of us sat on the edge of the locker behind the backstop and Dodger said, "Now that we're all mellowed out, tell us again about the thing with James Beeks."

So I told the story again. Then Dodger said, "You know, dude, maybe James didn't tell his dad to buy the forest."

"What are you talking about? Of course he did. First he was obnoxious about saving the forest, and then the next thing you know, his dad is buying it. What else could it mean?"

Rodger said, "Well, maybe he told his father about the project innocently, without evil intent. Perhaps James was just telling his father about the events of his day, and when the father heard about the forest, he got the idea to buy it on his own. For all you know, James feels terrible, awful, wracked with guilt about this."

I snorted. "Beeks feeling guilty? I don't think so."

Dodger said, "Or maybe the whole thing is, like, a coincidence. James happened to know about the forest, but his father found out about it some other way. I mean, if I eat a banana, and you already knew that bananas were a food, that doesn't mean I heard about them from you."

"Uh, that's a good point, but . . . he's James Beeks. He *lives* to mess up other people's plans. Plus, why are you both sticking up for him? He picks on me all the time, and now he's going to help destroy this whole place."

"I don't know," Rodger said. "I think that there is more to James Beeks than meets the eye. I think he has invisible depths, secret pains, hidden troubles. Anyway, what are you going to do next in your quest to save the forest?"

"Well, my dad wrote this book about how to be an activist, and Lizzie and I have been trying to follow the steps. The next one is Tell Truth to Power."

"Oh," Dodger said, "so you have to, like, sit in front of a light switch and confess all the bad things you've done?"

"No—it means you have to face whoever's in

charge and tell them that what's happening is wrong. You know, like Martin Luther King did. Or the Founding Fathers when they wrote the Declaration of Independence. So I think we're going to invite the mayor to a student council meeting and talk to him about the woods."

"Dude, I remember those meetings with Thomas Jefferson and those white-wigged guys!"

"Wow, I still can't believe you were there when the Declaration of Independence was written! What was it like?"

"Well, you know, it was made of yellowish paper, about a foot tall, with black ink all over it."

"No, I mean what was it like to *be* there?"

"Oh, you know: talk, talk, talk, write, write, write, talk, talk, talk, vote. Kind of ruined my July Fourth that year, actually."

"Yeah, but what was it like?"

"Mostly I remember wishing there were more snacks. Take my advice, Willie, if you want this mayor guy to listen, you have to have excellent munching items. I recommend a little chocolate, some fruit, and maybe something in a nice corn chip. If only those independence guys had stocked up beforehand,

I wouldn't have been out on a food run when they were all signing the paper. And then John Hancock wouldn't have written his name so big right in the spot I was supposed to sign."

"So," I said, "that's the best advice you two have? James Beeks isn't so bad, and snacks are good?"

"Pretty much," Dodger said. "Hey, got any bananas? All of this high-level political discussion really works up the old appetite."

"No bananas, sorry. How about you, Rodger? Any other words of wisdom?"

"Hmm . . . I'd say be careful when you brush your teeth. You have to really be sure you spend adequate time cleaning the back molars—a lot of people think the front teeth are most important, but you actually need all of your teeth to be healthy. So scrub, scrub, scrub! Buff, polish, rub, scour! Rinse! Spit! All right?"

"Rodger, how is brushing thoroughly going to help me save the woods?"

"It probably isn't. But there's no point to losing our home *and* having painful, unsightly cavities, is there?"

I guess he kind of had a point. I said good night and headed for home. As I stepped into the trees, I heard Rodger's voice calling after me: "And floss! You don't want to leave any disgusting, revolting, slimy particles of decaying foodstuffs to rot slowly between your teeth!"

When I got home, dinner was ready. But strangely, I wasn't all that hungry.

CHAPTER TEN

The Great Lasorda
and the Evil Beeks

THE NEXT DAY, Lizzie and I decided to pay a re-
turn visit to Lasorda. My mom almost didn't let us
go there alone, but then I reminded her that she was
supposed to be allowing me to express my independence. She said, "I just don't like knowing you and
Lizzie are going downtown to an adult's office alone."

"Well," I replied, "what if I bring your cell phone
and call you right before we go in and right after
we come out? And if you want, we could even do errands for you while we're out, or something." I could
tell she didn't exactly love the arrangement, but
she agreed. Every once in a while, those New Year's
resolutions came in handy.

Anyway, when Lizzie and I entered the waiting room, we could hear two voices through the door that led to the inner office. Lizzie was just about to knock, but I grabbed her arm and pulled her away. We sat down in a couple of chairs next to the door and listened for a while. It didn't take us long to figure out that the other voice belonged to Mr. Beeks. Here's what we heard:

LASORDA: You're sure you can pay cash for the property?

MR. BEEKS: Absolutely.

LASORDA: And you plan to leave it as open space, right?

MR. BEEKS: I never said that.

LASORDA: Yes, you did. When you looked at the land, you said, *I'm picturing nothing but green as far as the eye can see.*

MR. BEEKS: I didn't mean green like plants, I meant green like money.

Lasorda: Hmmm. Surely you don't plan to destroy everything. After all, you're calling the development Woodland Acres.

Mr. Beeks: That's traditional. Every builder I know does it—you name your development after whatever you knocked down to build it. My last three projects were called Piney Hills, Cherry Orchard Estates, and Stillwater Springs.

Lasorda: Well, it appears I did not fully understand your intentions.

Mr. Beeks: Are you trying to back out on me, mister? Because if you are, my lawyers will be all over you in a heartbeat. Since my grandfather, the first James Beeks, started our company, nobody has ever backed out of a deal with the Beeks family.

Lasorda: No, I am not backing out on you. Unfortunately, I have some . . . business debts to settle, so I have to sell the land.

(Just then someone knocked on the waiting room doorway from outside. Lizzie and I scrambled into a coat closet by the door and closed it behind us almost all the way. We could still hear the conversation, and through the crack in the door we could even see who had just walked in: James Beeks!)

MR. BEEKS: Good. You'll get your debts paid off, I'll get my new businesses going, and my lazy, worthless son will have a place to practice baseball.

LASORDA: And why did your son need his own private set of batting cages, again?

MR. BEEKS: Because last year, he choked in the clutch and blew his team's season.

LASORDA: I don't mean to pry, but isn't the boy only eleven years old? And didn't you tell me he only struck out once, in his last at bat of the season?

MR. BEEKS: Why, yes. But none of that matters. All that matters is that he failed. And the Beeks family does not believe in failure. So, next season he will not fail.

LASORDA: Is baseball really that important?

MR. BEEKS: Oh, it's not just baseball. He ran in his school election and lost, too. He needs to learn to be a winner before it's too late, and baseball is as good a place to start as any. The sooner those batting cages get built, the sooner I can make a man out of James.

(I couldn't believe James was standing there hearing this. He looked like he was about to cry.)

LASORDA: I . . . see. And are you sure the town government will allow you to flatten the woods? Will there not be protests from concerned citizens or environmental groups?

MR. BEEKS: Oh, there will be complaints. In fact, my son's little student council friends are planning to protest to the mayor and the town council. But they'll never win.

LASORDA: How can you be so sure?

MR. BEEKS: Because the mayor owes me some favors, just like everybody else who does business in this town. He's a good friend of mine. So I'll send the mayor to talk at the school. He'll listen to the little kiddies, he'll say thank you for your concern, I appreciate your citizenship, kids like you make me proud to be an American, blah, blah, blah. Maybe he'll even give the kids an award for community involvement or something. I have to admit, the mayor has a bit of an anger management problem, but how hard can it be to flatter a bunch of schoolchildren? Anyway, he'll listen to everything the kids have to say. But then, a few days later, the town will grant my building permit, anyway. By the time anybody figures out what happened, my bulldozers will have come and gone. And then nobody will say a thing about it—because I am a winner. I make things happen. I make money. And when I make money, this whole town makes money.

LASORDA: Is money really that important, Mr. Beeks?

MR. BEEKS: Would you be standing here talking to me now if it weren't?

At that moment, James turned and walked out of the waiting room. He slammed the door behind him, and Lasorda must have heard the noise, because he and Mr. Beeks stopped talking and stepped out of the office into the waiting room. They shook hands and said they would be in touch. Then Mr. Beeks left.

"You can come out now, children!" Lasorda said. Lizzie and I both jumped about two feet. Then Lasorda snapped his fingers and the closet door swung open. "Did you two hear that entire conversation?"

We both nodded. I mean, when an ancient, powerful genie busts you eavesdropping, what are you supposed to do?

"Good," Lasorda said. "*Very* good. Things are going just as I'd planned. I will pay off the leprechauns, and Dodger will still be in *my* debt. Although I do wish—oh, never mind!"

"What is it, Lasorda?"

"Well, it's just that sometimes I almost find myself wishing that Dodger still worked for me."

"Maybe you could talk to him and work something out," I said.

"I am the Great Lasorda," he replied. "I do not just *work something out* with my former employees."

"Hey, do you know who you sound like?" Lizzie asked him.

He thought for a moment, then flashed a tight, wicked grin. "If you say 'Mr. Beeks,' I may have to turn you into a tree or something. Now begone!"

Jeepers, just a second ago, Lasorda had been acting almost nice. Some people are *so* moody.

CHAPTER ELEVEN

Special Guests

THE NEXT STUDENT council meeting was a disaster. All week long in class, Mrs. Starsky kept hinting that we would have a special guest. She even took Lizzie, James, Craig, and me aside and warned us to be on our absolute best behavior for the meeting. I guess that made sense based on how much Lizzie and I usually argued with James and Craig, but ever since we had overheard that ugly conversation at Lasorda's office, I wasn't really mad at James anymore. I mostly just felt sorry for him. Anyway, we did try to behave at the meeting, but none of us could have known that there would be not one but two special guests.

Everything started off normally enough. I banged the gavel and called the council to order. Next Mrs. Starsky announced her guest. None of the other kids could believe it—she had gotten the mayor of the town to come to our meeting! Not only that but she promised we could make a presentation at the next town council meeting about why nobody should be allowed to build on the forest. I saw James Beeks mumbling under his breath when Mrs. Starsky said that, and Craig trying to calm him down. I glanced at Lizzie and saw that she wasn't paying any attention to Beeks and Flynn, because she was messing around with one of the school's laptop computers. That day for a science lesson, we had been making webcam videos about measurement, but I knew something had gone wrong with the RECORD button on the computer she was using. It was a shame, because the computer had an awesome built-in camera that let you record in any direction just by clicking on the track pad. If she could get the camera working again, it would really help her science grade. I didn't think she should be working on that right in front of the mayor, though—especially if he had anger issues. What if he got mad at us?

I forgot all about Lizzie's computer problem

when the mayor walked in. He strode through the door to the front of the classroom and immediately started in on a whole big speech: "It's great to see you kids taking an interest in our town's future, because you *are* the future. . . . If we all work together, we can accomplish miracles . . . blah, blah, blah." I don't know if it was just because of what Mr. Beeks had said about the mayor, but to me, the guy sounded even more phony than our principal. Except at least she didn't have a massive bald spot covered by the world's fakest-looking toupee. Still, he had our attention—until the really bad thing happened. All of a sudden, just as the mayor was saying, "If you apply the lessons of today, we can all have a brighter tomorrow," I saw a blue head pop around the corner of the doorway.

Oh, no, I thought. *Dodger, don't do this to me!* But then Dodger stuck a sign into the doorway. It said: SNAKS! Jeepers. Was he trying to tell me there were snakes in the room? Ugh, I hate snakes. But I looked around and didn't see any. Maybe he meant that there were snakes on the way to attack us? But I had never heard of snakes joining into a pack and swarming an elementary school. I shrugged at Dodger, just as the mayor was saying, "And I know you all love our wonderful country, right?"

Dodger pulled the sign back behind the door for a moment, and I realized the mayor was glaring at me for shrugging at the exact wrong moment. *Great*, I thought. *Now the mayor thinks I don't love my country.* Then Dodger's sign reappeared, with more words on it:

YU FORGOT THE SNAKS!

Oh, I thought. *Not snakes—snacks!* Dodger was right: I had totally forgotten to bring any snacks for our special guest. What was I going to do now? Dodger had obviously been serious about his thoughts on feeding people at meetings, but I had no idea he would actually show up at this event. Nobody but me and Lizzie could see Dodger or his signs, but if we didn't do anything, he might start making noise. And believe me, everybody can hear Dodger, even if they can't see him.

"Not now!" I hissed. Unfortunately for me, the mayor had just asked, "Will you all pledge to support your town, your state, and our beloved U.S. of A.?"

The mayor and everybody else stared at me. "Excuse me, son?" the mayor said. "Did you just say you won't support your town, your state, or your country?"

"Um, sorry, sir," I said. "I was just, uh, talking to someone else."

The mayor frowned, shook his head, and continued his speech. Meanwhile, Lizzie was elbowing me. "Get Dodger out of here," she whispered. I nodded. When Dodger peeked around the door frame again, I tried to shoo him away by gesturing with my hands under my desk.

Yeah, like Dodger was going to take a hint. Instead of leaving, he wrote another note:

I WIL JUST THROE THEM 2 YU!

Yikes! What was I going to do? If Dodger started throwing food to me, I was a dead man. Mrs. Starsky would completely flip out on me, the mayor would go ballistic, Beeks would never let me live it down, and I'd probably get kicked out of student council. Lizzie saw the note, too, and gasped.

I tuned in to the mayor for a second, and apparently he was reaching the climax of his patriotic speech. "Our flag," he said, "should always fly from

the highest heights! Long may it wave over moun-
tains and rivers, valleys and streams! Long may the
Stars and Stripes look down upon us from the blue
sky, giving us strength and courage!"

Oh, brother, I thought. *This is exactly what Mr. Beeks
said would happen. But what does any of this have to do
with saving the field?*

Dodger, meanwhile, was now holding some kind
of cream pie. It looked like he was getting ready to
lob the pie at me. Lizzie mouthed, *No, Dodger.* Then
she pointed at the floor and said, "On the ground!"
That wasn't a bad idea. At least if Dodger slid the
pie on the ground, the kids behind us wouldn't see it.
Plus, that way, I wouldn't be able to miss, and have
the pie splatter everywhere. I reached down below
my desk with both hands, preparing for Dodger to
slide the pie my way.

Sadly, the mayor had just asked, "And where
does our beautiful flag belong?"

Oopsie. Major oopsie. The mayor, and everyone
else, turned toward Lizzie and me. I was still all
bent over so that nobody could see my arms under
the desk, and Lizzie was looking over the mayor's
shoulder at Dodger. The mayor started to step over
to us. His foot was in the air as he said, "Young

lady, I don't know what is wrong with you and your friend there, but it will stop now! I will not have our country and our flag mocked like this. What is wrong with you? Where is your respect? And is that a foreign accent I hear?"

Lizzie looked like she was about to faint. *I wonder what she's going to say to that*, I thought. I never got a chance to find out, though, because just then, Dodger pushed the pie across the floor. The mayor's foot came down right in the middle of the spinning pastry, and he lost his balance. His foot slid out from under him, flinging the pie up in the air. Mrs. Starsky had been hurrying over to see what was going on—and she arrived at my desk just as the pie did.

SPLAT! We now had a teacher dripping with pie—banana cream pie, judging from the smell—and a very, very angry government official doing a split on the floor. The mayor spoke first, probably because he didn't have to spit out a big gob of whipped cream before he could make a sound. "You two are exactly what's wrong with America today. Foreigners and disrespectful brats!" He pointed at Lizzie and continued. "You come here and take our jobs. You don't respect our flag, our traditions, or our laws. If I had my way, everyone who wasn't born in the

U.S. would be sent back to their own country! Or thrown in jail forever!" Then he turned to me. "And you! Aren't you the president of this group?" I nodded weakly. "I came here because you wanted to save the forest and preserve the environment. Well, you know what? Nobody elected me to protect a bunch of trees! I couldn't care less about the environment! If it would help the most prominent citizens of this town to make money, I'd go out there and chop down those stupid trees myself!"

With that, the mayor stood up, dusted himself off, and stormed out of the room. As he reached the doorway, he turned and said, "If these students are the kind of leaders you produce here, I think this school should be closed down!"

I looked around. Most of the kids looked horrified. Except for James Beeks, who was grinning. *It figures*, I thought. *The second you start feeling sorry for a guy like Beeks—BAM!* Meanwhile, Mrs. Starsky was standing over Lizzie and me, with wads of banana pie goo dripping from her hair and face. "What on earth do you have to say for yourselves?" she demanded.

I gulped. There really wasn't much to say, was there?

I looked at Lizzie, who was looking down at her desk. No, I realized, she wasn't looking at the desk—she was looking at her laptop computer. And then I saw that the red RECORD light was blinking on her screen.

CHAPTER TWELVE

A Nice, Quiet Dinner with the Family

MRS. STARSKY SENT EVERYBODY other than Lizzie and me home, told us not to go anywhere, and went to the bathroom to get cleaned up. When she came back, she looked mostly normal—well, other than a little splotch of banana custard in her left eyebrow. But she was really, really angry at us.

At least, until Lizzie showed her the video of the speech on the laptop computer. Then Mrs. Starsky became really, really angry at the mayor. On the tape, you couldn't hear anything Lizzie or I had said, but you could tell we hadn't flung the pie. You could also see that the mayor had gone completely bonkers for very little reason. Mrs. Starsky made us swear that we hadn't thrown, pushed, bought, or even brought the pie (which was strictly true, anyway), and then apologized for the mayor's behavior. By the time we got out of there, Mrs. Starsky was just about ready to storm Town Hall by herself.

I hoped she'd get her eyebrow cleaned up first.

At dinner that night, Dad was really proud of himself. He was wearing a "Kiss the Cook" apron, and had made roast beef with potatoes and carrots on the side—the first time in my life I had ever seen him make anything other than eggs, toast, or grilled burgers. He told us he had even scrubbed off the top of the stove and washed the pots and pans already. Mom said, "Wow, that's some excellent manly housework!" Of course, that got Dad onto the topic of how our resolutions were going. I complimented Mom for letting me express my independence by going downtown with Lizzie to meet with Lasorda. Then I told the family about the upcoming town council meeting. Dad was thrilled that we were using his book as a guide for becoming activists, and wanted to know whether we had found a rare animal yet. I said we were working on it and that Lizzie and I planned to spend that Saturday morning searching the forest for endangered shrews, turtles, and squirrels. That was when the conversation started going downhill.

"Can I go? Huh? Huh?" Amy said. One thing you have to say for my sister: She never, ever gives up. Once she gets an idea, she's like a pit bull.

I had already tried yelling at Amy to make her stop following me and Lizzie around. I had even said mean things to her, and in fact, Amy hadn't talked to me for a few days. She probably didn't even want to spend time with me now, but she wanted to keep snooping. So she was trying to get my parents to make me take her along. The worst part was that they would probably fall for it.

"Mom, Dad," I pleaded. "Don't I deserve some privacy?"

"Ooh, Willers wants some privacy to be with his Lizzie-poo!"

"Be quiet, Amy!"

Amy smirked at me, but then put on her most innocent face and asked Dad, "But I want to help. I have a right to help. And aren't I supposed to stand up for my rights, Daddy?"

He looked unsure for a moment. Amy pushed on. "I mean, won't it be good for your book if I keep following my resolution?"

"Dad," I said, "you can't make us take her along! This is supposed to be *my* quest!"

"Then why are you taking Lizzie?" Amy said triumphantly.

That was it. I didn't have to sit there and listen to this. "Amy," I shouted, "you—are—not—going with us into the woods! You will never, ever be welcome to tag along with us! Now, for the last time, LEAVE ME ALONE!" Then I stormed upstairs. I don't know where all that grumpiness had come from all of a sudden. Maybe I was spending too much time with the mayor.

That Saturday morning was clear and beautiful. I put on some scruffy clothes and a pair of beat-up sneakers, in case we had to crawl around chasing animals. Then I met Lizzie at the edge of the woods, and we set out looking again for interesting creatures. I didn't see any Least Shrews, Flying Squirrels, or Bog Turtles, but I did see some strange flashes of green between the trees. When we got to a clearing, I stopped. "Lizzie," I muttered, "don't look, but I think we're being followed by leprechauns."

She giggled.

"I'm serious," I said. "I keep seeing green out of the corner of my eye, but when I turn around, they're gone."

"Hmm," Lizzie said, "maybe we can try to talk with them."

"Talk with them? Why would we want to do that?"

"Oh, come on, Willers. Think about it: If the forest gets chopped down, they're in a lot of trouble. Plus, Lasorda is only selling it so he can pay them back. Maybe we can get them on our side."

"I don't know, Lizzie. Dodger said they're tricky. And I happen to know they don't like it when people go looking for them."

"And how do you know that?"

"My mom read me this fairy tale once, and the prince in it tried to—"

"Willie, do you honestly mean to tell me you're afraid of leprechauns because of a fairy tale you once heard?"

Jeepers, when she said it that way, it sounded kind of wimpy. "All right," I said, "we can talk to the leprechauns. But how are we supposed to do that?"

"I dunno. Maybe we should make them an offering."

"An offering? Like what?"

"Let's see . . . what do leprechauns like?"

This was a really ridiculous conversation. But I actually did know something that leprechauns were supposed to like. I bent down, took off my right sneaker, and hopped into the middle of the clearing. I carefully placed the sneaker on a flat rock, hopped backward away from it, and sat down in the shade to wait.

"A sneaker?" Lizzie asked as she sat next to me. "Why would a magical forest creature care about your sneaker?"

"Ah," I said, "it's not just any old sneaker. It's a sneaker with a broken lace and a worn-out heel. Leprechauns fix shoes."

"Why?"

"It's what they do, that's all."

"So you're leaving them a smelly old piece of athletic footwear—damaged athletic footwear. That sounds kind of crazy, don't you think?"

I thought for a second, then burst out in a fit of giggles. Here we were, trying to save a forest so that our magical chimpanzee friend wouldn't lose his home. The land was being sold by a genie, and now we were attempting to lure a leprechaun into a meadow. And Lizzie thought the broken sneaker was the crazy part?

Lizzie said, "I don't really see what's so fu—" Then she had to stop talking, because the giggles overcame her, too. We laughed until we were doubled over, gasping for breath. When we finally recovered and sat up again, there was a little man standing next to my sneaker. And when I say little, I'm serious; the guy must have been a foot and a half tall. He had bright red hair and was wearing a very old-fashioned green suit with black buckle shoes and a matching buckled hat. He was studying the sneaker the way a doctor looks at an injury: peering at it from all angles, poking around it gently, and saying *hmmm* . . . a lot.

I cleared my throat. The little man jumped back a step and shouted, "Hark! Who dares deface this meadow with such an unflattering, odorous specimen of low-quality footwear?"

"Well, sir, I didn't mean to offend you with it. My name is Willie, and this is my best friend, Elizabeth.

We just wanted to meet you because . . . well, we're trying to save this forest from being sold and destroyed. We thought maybe you, uh, wee people might want to help us."

"Wee people? Wee people? Ye think we are wee? Well, we are not wee, are we? Nay, lad, we are the large, powerful, and mighty leprechauns. I am known as Big Pat Clancy, but if that's too much to say, ye can just call me Big."

"Um, okay, Big. Would you like to help us save the forest?"

"Wait a moment, son," Big said. He had taken a little pair of eyeglasses from his vest pocket and slipped them on. "I just need to concentrate so I can operate on this sorry excuse for a shoe."

Sorry excuse for a shoe? That shoe happened to be the exact same model worn by my absolute favorite basketball player. I knew because I had seen the commercials. I didn't say anything, though.

The examination continued. "Uh-huh, cracked leather here. Worn rubber down there. And is this some torn . . . plastic? Honestly, how shabby. Even back in the days when I was but a large and formidable apprentice, I knew better than to make a shoe out of plastic. Would ye make a wedding ring out of

110

tin? Would ye make a cake out of rocks? Would ye make a rainbow out of bubble gum?"

"Um, no, sir?"

" 'No, sir' is right!"

"So you can't fix it, then?" Lizzie asked.

"Can't fix it? Are ye kiddin' me, lass? There isn't a shoe made that I can't fix! I just hate wasting my talents on this piece o' rubbish, that's all. But if ye really want me to, I'll do it. Now, Willie, do ye want this lace repaired?"

I nodded.

Big Pat Clancy reached behind his ear and somehow pulled a sparkling, brand-new shoelace out of the air. He mumbled, "Better replace the pair, then," and created another lace. Then he tapped his finger on the sneaker, and instantly, one of the new laces had replaced my old, torn one. Lizzie tapped my shoulder and pointed down at the foot that still had my other sneaker on it. That one had a new lace as well—and I had never felt a thing!

Pretty cool.

Big nodded with satisfaction. "Would ye like me to repair the wear and tear on the rest of this shoe, then?" I nodded.

"And the other one?" I nodded again.

"Better give 'er over, then, laddie." I took off the other sneaker and walked across the grass to give it to him. Yuck! The dew soaked through my socks and drenched my feet. I trudged back to sit next to Lizzie again. "Now cover your eyes—this next part is too brilliant for your mortal minds!"

I wasn't sure how brilliant shoe cleaning— even magical shoe cleaning—could be, but I covered my eyes. Lizzie covered hers, too. We sat that way for a minute. As far as I could tell, nothing was happening. But the minute stretched into two minutes, then three. Finally, Lizzie couldn't take the silence anymore, so she said, "Mr. Clancy? Um, Big? Sir?"

There was no response. I peeked out from behind my hand and saw that the little man was gone. My sneakers were sitting on the rock, but Mr. Big was nowhere in sight. I turned to Lizzie and saw that she had peeked, too. We walked over to the sneakers and checked them out. I had to admit, even if he had just been using them to distract us and disappear, the repair job was pretty sweet. They were now spotlessly, blindingly white in the sunlight, and instead of their old slightly funky aroma, they now gave off a strong lemon-fresh scent.

"Hey, look!" Lizzie said, pointing to the side of one sneaker. Where there had been the swooshy sort of stripe that the manufacturer used as a trademark, now each shoe had a fluorescent-green shamrock.

That was either really cool, or the dorkiest thing I had ever seen.

Anyway, I put the sneakers on. They felt great—somehow they now fit better, and my feet were practically tingling with happiness. "Oh, well," I said. "If the leprechauns aren't going to help save the forest, at least I got some free shoe-repair work out of the deal."

Lizzie frowned. "Why would he just disappear like that?"

"I have no idea. Maybe he really was offended by my sneaker?"

"No, there must have been something else. Here, let's try to get him back." She took off her left boot, placed it on the stone, and shouted, "Mr. Big! Come back! Please!"

We closed our eyes for a second, and when we

reopened them, there he was. But now he looked furious! "So, I see how it is! The so-called Great Lasorda sent ye, didn't he?"

"No," I said. "What are you talking about? Why are you so angry all of a sudden?"

"I know he sent ye. Not only do ye have his hideous taste in footwear but ye're sneaky like he is, as well."

"What do you mean?" Lizzie asked.

"As if ye didn't know, missy. I mean that while ye had me here, working on your stinking excuse for a shoe, your accomplice was snooping around the forest behind my back! From what I hear, she's already been and gone while ye had me slaving away at the thankless task of mending your shoe. Well, take *this*, then!" He tapped Lizzie's boot, which melted into a sad puddle of rubber. "Now, get out of here, and consider yourselves lucky I don't use my mighty charms and spells to do even worse! As for me, I'm off to gather my allies around me and confront your little sidekick! Look out behind you!"

We both whirled to look, but it was just a trick. When we turned back around, Big Pat Clancy was gone.

"Um, sorry about the boot, Lizzie."

"Never mind the boot, Willie. Don't you know what must have happened?"

I thought about it. *Snooping . . . little accomplice . . .* "Amy!" I shouted.

Lizzie kicked off her lone remaining boot. Then we ran all the way to my house.

CHAPTER THIRTEEN

Nothing a Gallon or Two of Mouthwash Won't Fix

YOU KNOW YOU'RE HAVING a bad day when kissing a frog isn't even the bad news—but this was rapidly turning into that kind of day. By the time Lizzie and I burst into the back door of my house, I had no idea what we would find—but I had a feeling I wouldn't like it. I yelled for my parents, and they didn't answer. Then I remembered my father saying he was going downtown to rent a pressure washer and something called a Shop-Vac. Apparently, manly housekeeping is more fun if you use complicated, expensive power tools. *And Hey*, I thought, *maybe Mom took Amy out on some errands or something. Maybe everything is fine after all.*

Also, if my family wasn't in the house, I could yell for some magical help. "DODGER," I shouted, "WE'RE HOME!"

There was no reply. That was somewhat unusual.

"Hmm . . . he must be taking a nap," I said. Dodger is a big, big fan of naps.

"Or in his lamp." Lizzie was right: Dodger spends a lot of his free time in his lamp. Anyway, Lizzie and I started up the stairs to see what Dodger was up to, but stopped short when we heard a weird croaking noise coming from behind the closed door of Amy's room. "Did you hear that?" I asked Lizzie.

She looked a little nervous. "Umm, was it, like, an odd crick-crick sort of sound?"

"Yeah."

"Sort of frog-ish sounding?"

"Yeah."

"Nope," she said. "Can't say I heard anything like that. Listen, do you want to go outside and play tag or something? Right *now*?"

"Lizzie, what are you talking about? Don't you want to see what's going on in my sister's room?"

"Well, I prob'ly haven't mentioned this before, but I have a little, um, problem with frogs."

117

"Problem? What kind of problem?"

"They . . . they make me kind of . . . well . . . *sick*."

Just then, there was a whole series of croaks, followed by a hollow thumping noise. It sounded like a large frog was throwing itself at Amy's door from the inside. "All right," I said, "why don't you stay here? I'll just check out what's going on, and you can run for help if things get ugly. Deal?"

We heard several "ribbits," each of which was followed by a solid THUNK. Lizzie looked as though she might faint. She nodded. "Don't worry, Willie," she said bravely. "I've got your back. Just as long as I don't have to touch a frog."

I turned and crept up the last few stairs. Then I tiptoed to Amy's door, gently turned the knob, and pushed my way in. I put one foot slightly in front of the other, like the karate fighters in my favorite video game. I balled my hands into fists. I was ready for anything.

Anything except what I found in there. Amy's room was trashed! Her bedcovers were thrown around, her dresser drawers were all pulled open, and her stuff was tumbled out all over the place. Worst of all, there was a big, slimy frog crashing itself into my left foot repeatedly. Bending down to take a closer look, I noticed that the frog had a sort of bluish tint. Also, he appeared to be wearing a black eye patch.

"Oh, no!" I said, my voice shaking. "Lizzie, come quick!"

"You mean, come quick*ly*," she replied. "Anyway, is everything all right?"

"Not exactly," I said.

"But there isn't actually a frog in there, is there?"

"Not exactly."

She bounded up the steps and into the room. Then she looked down, saw the frog, and gasped. "Not exactly?" she asked. "Then what do you call *that*?"

I sat down on Amy's bed and sighed. "I'm pretty sure I call it *Dodger*."

Lizzie bent down to take a closer look, studied the blue-green amphibian that was now jumping up and down on top of my foot, and said, "Oh, dear." Then she straightened up and charged out of the room in the direction of the bathroom.

From the sound of things, she made it there in time. But barely.

By the time she got back, looking kind of pale

and sickly, I was on my hands and knees checking out something on the floor. Amy kept a big glass jar of seashells on her dresser, but it had been knocked over onto the floor, and the shells were all spilled out onto the floor. At first I had thought the shells were just spread out randomly, but then I noticed that a lot of them had been pushed into patterns to make letters. The letters looked like this: SS ME LIZZY

Lizzie bent down next to me and read the letters, too. I turned to her and said, "Lizzie, do you know what this is? It's a message from Dodger! He's trying to tell us—"

Lizzie laughed. " 'Toss me Lizzy'? What the heck does that mean? Are we supposed to find some girl named Lizzy and throw her at him? And how is *that* supposed to help?"

I looked at her in disbelief. She was usually much quicker than I was at figuring things out. How could she not see this? "It doesn't say 'Toss me Lizzy'!" I said.

Meanwhile, the Dodger frog was jumping up and down, like it wanted to get our attention. We both looked and saw that he had pushed a longish, slightly curved shell into place between the second and third groups of letters, which now said this: SS ME, LIZZY

She frowned. " 'Pass me, Lizzy'? Like a football? Wouldn't that be, um, animal cruelty?"

I said, "It doesn't say 'Pass me, Lizzy,' either. It says—"

" 'Miss me, Lizzy'? I still don't get it."

"Lizzie, quit messing around! It means 'KISS me, Lizzy'! You know what they say about frogs and magic—that you have to kiss them to turn them back into their original form? Well, I bet you have to kiss the frog so he can turn back into Dodger!"

Lizzie looked like she was going to pass out any second, but she wasn't done arguing yet. "No, it's clearly not meant to be me, Willie. My name is spelled with an '-ie' at the end, NOT a '-y.' Must be a different person altogether."

This was too much. "Lizzie!" I said. "You know Dodger can't spell. Of *course* it means you." Dodger jumped up and down again when I said this, and I could have sworn he was glaring at me. Although when you're talking about a one-eyed frog, it's kind of hard to be 100 percent sure.

I looked at Lizzie. She was glaring at me, too. And her lower lip was trembling a little. "Willie, I can't," she said. "I'm . . . afraid!"

Holy cow. Lizzie was never afraid of anything. "Really?"

"Yes, really! When I was only four or five years old, back in England, my rich, horrible old aunt had me over for dinner one night. She served me these little fried things that looked like chicken wings. I didn't want to try them, because she had once tried to feed me snails. But then she said I couldn't have dessert unless I ate one. And the dessert was this huge, lovely cake with swirly whipped cream on top. And cherries. You know, those really bright-colored ones that are cut in half? I love those. Plus, all the grown-ups were looking at me, and it was embarrassing. So I picked up one of the fried things and took a little nibble."

"And?"

"And it was delicious! I ate every bit of meat off of the bone. Then I grabbed another one and ate that one, too. I swear, I must have eaten seven or eight of the things before I stopped to take a break. That was when some old man grinned at me, leaned over across the table, and said, 'Do you know what you're eating?' 'No,' I said. 'Chicken wings?' He laughed a wicked laugh and said, 'Not quite, child. Those are frog's legs!' "

"Wow. What happened then?"

Lizzie looked down and away from me, like she was embarrassed. Meanwhile, I couldn't help but notice that Dodger had kind of crab-walked around to the side of me where Lizzie wasn't, as though he was afraid she might grab him for a snack.

"I felt nauseated all of a sudden, right? So I knew I had to get out of there, pronto. I jumped up out of my seat and tried to make a run for it, but one of my aunt's maids was wheeling the dessert trolley into place behind me. I smashed into it and—"

"And?"

"And threw up all over the cake!"

I looked at her for a minute. She played with the hem of her shirt. Dodger tried to crawl under Amy's bed. Then I said, as gently as I could, "You know you have to do this, right?"

Lizzie looked miserable and angry at the same time. "*Have* to do it? And my mum always says we moved here because America is a free country. Hah!"

"Come on," I said. "You can do this. I'll grab Dodger and bring him to the bathroom. We can pour some mouthwash into a glass and have it right there ready for you. One little peck and it'll all be over. How bad can it be?"

Lizzie sighed. She knew there was no choice. I mean, if your friend got stuck in a frog's body, you'd pucker up and give him a big old kiss right on the slimy lips to break the spell, right?

Right?

I coaxed Dodger out from under the bed and carried him to the bathroom, which looked clean—apparently, Lizzie had finished her previous mad dash in time. Lizzie followed. I put Dodger down on the counter and poured Lizzie about half a glass of mouthwash. She looked at the mouthwash, then at me. I tried to look encouraging as Lizzie took a deep breath, crossed her fingers for luck, and leaned over to kiss a frog.

CHAPTER FOURTEEN

Kiss and Tell

JUST AS LIZZIE GOT HER FACE all the way down to his level, Dodger kind of scootched backward a few inches. Lizzie rolled her eyes. "Dodger," she said, "I promise I'm not going to eat your legs, okay? Now, can we get this over with?"

I don't think frogs have necks, but somehow Dodger gave the impression that he was shaking his head at us. Then he raised his front leg and pointed it at the glass of mouthwash.

Lizzie giggled nervously. "Oh, Dodger, you're worried about kissing me without using mouthwash first? How sweet! Here, I'll, uhh, soak a cotton ball with the mouthwash. Then we can squeeze it over your face, and you can stick out your tongue to get some in your—"

But Dodger jumped backward. He was clearly shaking his head again. He pointed at Lizzie.

She got mad. "Wait, you want ME to use mouth-wash before I kiss YOU? I'll have you know I have very fresh breath. In fact, I just rinsed my mouth with toothpaste in this very bathroom just a few minutes ago. But here: If it will get this over with faster, I'll be glad to oblige your ridiculous, pig-headed request."

She grabbed the mouthwash and took a big swig. "Um, not to be too technical about it or anything," I said, "but I think it was actually a frog-headed request."

Apparently, that wasn't the right time to make a joke, because Lizzie and Dodger both gave me dirty looks again. Then, before any of us had time to think, Lizzie grabbed Dodger with one hand, lifted him to her lips, and gave him a kiss. She put him down on the counter. Then she washed her mouth out about fifty times, and scrubbed her hands with hot water and tons of soap.

Just as Lizzie turned to get a hand towel from the rack, there was a loud POP! All of a sudden, the frog on the counter turned into a blue chimpanzee. A four-and-a-half-foot-tall chimpanzee. His head whacked into the bathroom ceiling with a terrible hollow thump, like what you'd get if you whacked a coconut with a board. His one visible eye rolled up into his head, and he fell straight backward off the counter.

I hurled myself toward the edge of the counter-top and tried to catch Dodger, but he outweighed me by at least sixty pounds, so we both went tumbling over the edge of the tub. Dodger landed on top of me so hard that I couldn't breathe. While I struggled to get some air into my lungs, Lizzie started shouting, "Oh, my goodness! Dodger, are you all right? And Willie? Willie, can you hear me? Please, Willie, say something—anything!"

I felt Dodger stirring. Slowly, he pushed himself up and off me. Then he turned, grabbed me by the arms, and hoisted me out of the tub. I looked at him. Lizzie looked at me. He looked at Lizzie. Although he was still looking kind of dazed and was rubbing the top of his head with one hand, he sounded like he was back to normal as he said, "So, Lizzie, am I a great kisser, or what?"

She elbowed him in the ribs and said, "I swear

to you, Dodger, if I get warts on my face from this, I'll—"

"Wait a minute, you two!" I said. "Dodger, what happened? Where's my sister?"

Just then, there was a POOF! and Rodger appeared next to Lizzie. The bathroom was getting rather crowded. "Dodger," he said, "did you send out a distress call? Are you all right, safe, A-Okay, peachy-keen, hunky-dory—?"

Dodger put his other hand on his head and sat down next to me on the edge of the tub. "No, I'm not okay. Dudes, it was horrible! I tried to protect Amy, but they zapped me too fast. And there were so many of them. They burst into the house without even knocking. They were screaming and yelling at each other, blowing whistles, barking orders that didn't make any sense as they came clumping up the stairs. Amy was in her room, and they stormed straight in there and started bossing her around. I tried to talk to them, but they wouldn't listen to anyone but themselves. They had no mercy. They had no pity. They had really clunky, old-fashioned footwear!"

"Oh, no," Rodger exclaimed. "It can't be! Willie's sister has been kidnapped—by a bunch of elementary-school principals?"

"Worse than that, Rodger." He took a deep, shuddering breath, and I could see Rodger wondering what in the world could be scarier than a pack of principals.

Then Rodger said, "Lunch ladies?"

Ugh. That *would* be worse. But Dodger shook his head.

"No, bro, I *wish* it had been lunch ladies. But it's even more totally horrible-riffic than that."

"Dodger," Lizzie said, "I don't think 'horrible-riffic' is a word, actually."

"Can we please focus?" I asked. "Dodger, just tell us: Who took my sister?"

Dodger shuddered and said, "Sprites, Rodger. The dreaded sprites."

"Sprites? Amy was kidnapped by a group of sodas?"

Lizzie chimed in. "No, Rodger. Sprites are mythical woodland creatures. You know, pixies, elves, fairies . . ."

"Leprechauns," Dodger added.

"All right," I asked, "so what's so scary about the leprechauns? They're only, like, a foot and a half tall."

Dodger fired back, "The leprechauns might be

small, but they're totally tough. And tricky—if you look away from one for even a second, he goes POOF!"

Yes, we had already noticed that. "All right, so what happened after they came in?"

"I told you, they zapped me and I turned into a frog. They also cast a Shoe Spell on your mom."

"A Shoe Spell?"

"Yes, the dreaded Curse of the Comfortable High Heel. Your mom is sitting downstairs now, staring at a magical, perfectly comfortable high-heeled shoe—hypnotized. Don't worry, she'll be fine once we wake her up, although she may develop a strange dissatisfaction with all of her dress shoes. Anyway, then they grabbed Amy. Their leader guy kept saying, 'She is the chosen one! She is the cho-sen one!' She was kicking and yelling, but they did some kind of magic spell thing and she fell asleep. The next thing I knew, like, twelve of the little dudes picked her up on their shoulders and carried her out the door. I tried to go after them, but I couldn't turn the doorknob!"

"So what DID you do?"

Dodger looked a little sheepish. "I, um, ate a fly."

Lizzie's eyebrows shot up. "You ATE a fly?"

"Dude, for your information, flies happen to be delicious. They have this thin, crunchy outer coating, and then on the inside there's this juicy, zesty burst of flavor!"

Lizzie just looked at him.

"What? Was I supposed to just let him fly around annoying everybody all day? And waste all those essential vitamins and minerals?"

I cleared my throat, and they both looked at me. "Okay, so what are we going to do about this?"

"Um, wash it down with some fruit juice?"

"No, Dodger, what are we going to do about the fact that ANGRY FAIRY CREATURES HAVE MY SISTER?"

"Oh, that," Dodger said. "Why didn't you say so? Uh, the way I see it, all we have to do is find their place of power, round up some magical weapons, attack, and get Amy back. No problemo."

"I see," I said through clenched teeth. "All we have to do is attack the leprechauns in their headquarters. Even though we're totally outnumbered and don't know what the heck we're doing. Or where the headquarters even *is*."

"Sure, when you say it like *that*, it sounds pretty bad. But we totally know where their hideout is."

Lizzie and I both said, "We do?"

"Duh—at the end of the rainbow."

"So all we have to do is wait for it to rain, hope the sun comes out at the perfect time, and go for it?"

"Well," Dodger said, "that would work. But it's not the easiest way."

I stomped my foot. "NO FOOLING!" I shouted. "But do you have a better idea?"

"Sure, we could just walk there in, like, ten minutes flat."

"What are you talking about? It isn't even raining." I couldn't believe we were even talking about this like it made some kind of sense. But my life is just kind of weird like that, I guess.

Dodger took a deep breath and said, "Can you name the colors of the rainbow, Willie?"

"Yeah, we learned them in art class. Red, orange, yellow, green . . . ummm . . ."

Lizzie took over: "Blue, indigo, violet."

"Right. And what color is the Field of Dreams?"

"Blue," I said. "So what?"

"So if we just go to the Field of Dreams, and then go to the next, next field, that's where the leprechauns will be."

"The next field?" Lizzie asked.

"No, not the next field—that would be indigo. We have to go to the *next*, next field. Boy, do I have to explain everything? Two colors after blue is violet. And that's the end of the rainbow. So all we have to do is get to the purple field."

I swear, if Dodger ever *starts* making sense to me, I think I'll go get my head examined. But hey, if we were going to go get ourselves into a huge mess of trouble and danger, at least the location was convenient.

"All righty, then," I said. "All we have to do is walk over there with some—what do you call 'em?— magical weapons, attack the leprechauns, and save my sister. Good thing that's not a completely terrifying idea or anything."

"Dude, you don't need to worry."

"I don't?" I asked.

"He doesn't?" Rodger asked.

"Nope," Dodger said with a goofy grin. Then he said the five scariest words in the English language: "I totally have a plan!"

CHAPTER FIFTEEN

We Invade the End of the Rainbow

SO NOW YOU KNOW how I ended up on a snow-board with Dodger, flying off a ski jump and over the rainbow in order to save my sister. It was a crazy ride. I think I would have had trouble just riding a regular board down the magical mountain that Dodger had created in the middle of the Field of Dreams. But when the board was painted with flying potion, and I had a hyperactive chimp cling-ing to my back, things got really difficult.

Somehow we didn't wipe out on the downhill, al-though that meant we had developed some seriously terrifying speed going into the slalom course. Before I even knew what was going on, Dodger started leaning sideways and shouting, "Right! Now left! Now right again!" in my ear. I twisted my body one way, then the other, then back again, and—miraculously—we made it through the slalom flags, too.

Which only left the scariest part of all: the jump. "All right, Willie!" Dodger yelled. "We just have to make sure we get enough height to go over the rainbow. If we hit it—"

I could feel him shudder even in the middle of zipping down the ramp. "What happens if we hit the rainbow?"

"Um—let's just not do that, dude. Okay?"

Yikes. We went down the rest of the ramp so fast that it felt like the skin on my face was going to peel off. I leaned forward as hard as I could, even though every nerve in my whole body was screaming STOP! at full volume. I knew we only had one shot at this, and I had to rescue Amy.

Going off the end of the ramp was the most nauseating thing that's ever happened to me. It was like my stomach had dropped straight down through my body and tumbled away into space. Only worse. We flew upward so hard that my feet were getting crushed against the board. We were higher than the treetops of the forest. We were nearly as high as the clouds! Then, just when I felt like I might faint, we reached the top of our arc through the air—and started drifting downward. There was a rainbow about fifty feet ahead of us and maybe twenty feet down. I couldn't tell whether we were going to clear the top of it.

"PULL UP!" Dodger yelled. Whatever that meant.

I tried hard to lift my front foot in its strap, and that seemed to add a little lift to our glide. Then we were maybe twenty feet from the rainbow and ten feet above it. I pulled up even harder, and felt Dodger bouncing on the end of the board behind me. The front of the board angled even higher, and we cleared the rainbow by maybe six inches, at the most.

Whew. I didn't know what happens when you hit a rainbow on a snowboard, but I was glad this wouldn't be my day to find out. "What now?" I asked Dodger over the roar of the wind in my ears.

"Now comes the crash landing! Hang on!" Yeah, like he really needed to tell me to hang on. Although, come to think of it, what was I supposed to hang on *to*? I didn't have long to wonder, because the next thing I knew, we were losing altitude faster than ever. Suddenly, the bottom of the board was smashing through branches. Then we were tumbling forward. I did at least three somersaults when I hit the ground, which hurt pretty badly. Then Dodger landed on top of me, which hurt even worse.

I groaned, spat out a twig, and sat up. Dodger climbed off my back and said, "Cool, huh?" Strangely, it *was* kind of cool—not that you should try it at home or anything. But then I looked up. The scene in front of me was unbelievable: There were approximately thirty leprechauns standing around a bonfire. Sitting in a wooden chair in front of the blaze was my sister, Amy. Her eyes widened when she saw me. All the leprechauns were staring, too. Then one, who was even shorter than the others, stomped up to us and said, "I am Tim Tuttle, the Improbably Large. I rule this land. Ye dare to invade our magical glade with only two warriors? Are ye insane?"

"Dude, who said there were only two of us?" Dodger said. At that exact moment, Lizzie and Rodger came plummeting from the sky on the Magic Carpet of Khartoum and landed on top of Tim Tuttle. As a tiny bump under a carpet, he didn't look so improbably large at all. His voice was pretty big, though. "'Et 'e oug ub here!" he shouted through the thick rug. "'Et 'e oug ub here!"

"What's that you say? Get you out of there?" Rodger said. "I think we can grant you that wish, perform that task, render that service. Hang on!" Rodger and Lizzie jumped off the carpet, then reached down and lifted the edge.

Tim Tuttle climbed out from beneath the rug, spitting out dust bunnies and sneezing. Then he said, "Leprechauns! Attack! Attack! At-choo!"

The leprechauns were standing around looking confused. "Who's At-choo?" one of them asked. "And why would we attack him?" asked another. Finally, Big Pat Clancy stepped out of the throng and said, "A-ha! I should have known it was ye, Dodger! And ye, Rodger! And ye, Willie of the Stinky Sneakers!"

"And me," Lizzie said, stepping toward him. "Lizzie of the Melted Boot!"

I stepped up next to her. "Let my sister go," I said in my strongest, steadiest voice.

"Who's your sister, Stinky?"

I pointed to Amy. "That's her, right there! The one you're holding hostage. We tried to be friends with you before. We tried to be nice and reasonable. But if you want a fight, I'll fight every single one of you to get my sister back!"

Amy jumped up. "You will?" she asked, sounding surprised.

Truthfully, I was kind of surprised at what I'd said, too. But as soon as I had said it, I'd known it was true. "I will!" I said, raising my fists.

"Wait a minute," Tim Tuttle said. "Your sister is our new queen?"

"No, I'm telling you, my sister is that girl right there—Amy!"

Right when I said "Amy," every leprechaun dropped to one knee and chanted, "Long may she reign!"

Whoa. Apparently, my sister *was* their new queen. Tim Tuttle said, "It is rather unfortunate that ye are the brother of Queen Amy—long may she reign. Now I can't order my entire army to attack ye."

I breathed a sigh of relief.

But then Tim Tuttle continued, "As a nobleman by blood, ye are entitled to death by single combat instead!"

So much for the relief. I forced myself to sound braver than I felt. "Oh, yeah? Who's gonna fight me?"

Tim Tuttle called three leprechauns out of the group: "Stand forward, Hank O'Hare, the Extremely

Long-Armed. Stand forward, Nick Shea of the Bulging, Sculpted Biceps. Stand forward, Walter O'Malley of the, Um, Really Huge Teeth."

"Wait a minute! If it's single combat, how come I have to fight three of you?"

Lizzie said, "Yeah! I mean, I know your people are a bit on the small side, but—"

"Small side?" Tim Tuttle thundered. "SMALL SIDE?"

I reached over and pinched Lizzie's arm. "You're not helping," I hissed.

"We shall see who is on the small side, Willie!" screamed Tuttle. "Attack!"

I spread my feet and made my hands into fists, just like they do in my Ultimate Fighting video game. I tried to look as intimidating as I could, and prepared to die in battle for my sister. Or at least get hit in the shins a lot.

But then Amy yelled: "STOP!"

Everyone stopped. The leprechauns stopped because she was their queen, and the rest of us stopped because Amy is just so darn loud when she really wants to be. She stood and walked over between me and the three wee fighting men. "Nobody has to fight today," she said. "We're all on the same side."

"We are?" Tim Tuttle asked.

"We are?" Dodger repeated.

"Yes. Willie, aren't you trying to save the wild and magical forest?"

I nodded.

"Tim Tuttle, aren't you trying to save the wild and magical forest, too?"

Sheepishly, he nodded as well.

"Then there's no time to waste! We have to sit down together and figure out a way to make this happen. Men, bring out my book!" Two leprechauns came forward, holding a copy of Dad's classic *Save the Planet in Ten Easy Steps*. "I think what we are up to now is Step Four: Identify your allies. Then comes Step Five: Brainstorm a list of your assets."

"Our what?" I asked.

Rodger said, "Assets. You know, tools. Weapons. Things we have going for us."

"After that, we'll go to Step Six: Plan your presentation, followed by Step Seven: State your case in public."

"Wait," I said. "Before we start, can somebody please tell me how my sister became your queen?"

"It's somewhat embarrassing, actually," Big Pat Clancy said. "Ye were right that we went to your house intending to take her hostage. But as soon as we burst into her room, she said we had better stand back or her brother's blue ape friend would attack us. We asked what blue ape friend she was talking about, and she said, 'I don't know who he is, but I know that if he's a friend of my brother's, he won't let anything happen to me.' We asked where he was, and she said she didn't know because she couldn't see him. That was when we knew that Amy—long may she reign—had to be our queen."

"Huh? Why?" I asked.

"Because your sister has the greatest gift a human can have. Ye first believed in magical creatures because ye could see Dodger, right?"

"Yeah, I guess so."

"Willie, it's easy to believe in magic if you can see it. But your sister believed even though she could NOT see—and even when you kept telling her she was wrong. Your sister has true faith in the power of magic. And that is what the world needs most from you humans. If all of you trusted in the unseen power of magic, the wild places of the world wouldn't be disappearing. And my people could still roam free, granting our mighty blessings wherever we go. So we made Amy—long may she reign—our queen, and granted her the power to see the magic in the world."

I looked at my sister, who nodded. "I knew you were hanging out with an invisible blue orangutan. I just knew it! You lied to me!" Then she looked at Dodger and shyly said, "Um, hello."

Dodger grinned sheepishly and said, "Hi, Amy."

"Hey, I didn't exactly lie," I said. "Technically, he's a chimpanzee." She still looked hurt, so I continued. "But I'm sorry I didn't trust you, Amy."

She ran over and hugged me, then stepped away. "All right," she said. "What are we all standing around for? We've got a forest to save!" Then we all sat down in a big circle and got to work.

CHAPTER SIXTEEN

The Big Meeting

WHEN AMY AND I got home several hours later, we woke up our mom, who was totally fine—although I have noticed she's been spending a lot of time looking at shoe catalogs lately. Then we sat down to make some more plans for the big city council meeting. In fact, Lizzie, Amy, and I spent basically every free moment for the next few weeks working on our presentation—with the student council during the days, and with our magical friends after school. Then, finally, the big day came. I could hardly sit still in class, and it looked like Mrs. Starsky was having the same problem. She kept asking us over and over, "Are you sure you're ready? And do you promise you won't cause another big scene like you did with the mayor? Because I'm telling you, we just can't have that again."

I looked her right in the eye and said, "We're ready." I didn't promise not to cause a big scene, because frankly, I thought that would be one promise I would have to break.

My parents drove Amy and me to Town Hall for the meeting. I was all dressed up in my only suit. I hadn't worn it since my cousin Theresa's wedding the year before, and the arms and legs had gotten kind of short on me. But Dad's book said it was important to dress up if you wanted the "people in suits" to take you seriously. Lizzie was already at the front of the big room when we got there, setting up her laptop for the very special slide show we'd been working on. If the leprechauns and Rodger did their jobs when the time came, that slide show was going to be amazing.

The mayor was near the front of the room, too, chatting with Mr. Beeks. They were smiling at each other nonstop, and there was lots of backslapping and handshaking going on. It looked like they thought the building project was a done deal. But we had other ideas.

The hall filled up shockingly fast. All of the student council members were there with their parents, and so were a whole bunch of reporters and a lot of other grown-ups. Lizzie and Rodger had written a couple of letters to the newspapers, and Mrs. Starsky had put one of them in our school's monthly newsletter. Apparently, adults really read that stuff, because they were showing up in droves. There were also dozens of leprechauns around the room. Some were sitting on light fixtures, some were perched on the balcony railings, and some were just standing around. Even the Great Lasorda was in the room, wearing his most sparkling golden outfit.

It's amazing what people don't notice.

The mayor started the meeting. He looked like he wanted to grab me and Lizzie and shake us, but of course he couldn't do that in public. Instead he just told the crowd, "Thank you all for coming tonight. As you know, recently the parcel of vacant land behind our elementary school was sold by one private citizen to another. Even though we as a town believe that the government should try *very* hard not to interfere in private, legal business, *some* youngsters in this town feel otherwise." He paused to glare at Lizzie and me, then continued. "These chil-

146

dren have put together a little slide show in an attempt to show us why they feel the land should remain vacant. After the presentation, the city council will vote on whether the town should withhold the building permit that Mr. James Beeks, Senior, has requested for the property. Are there any questions?"

Ooh, this was going to be good! We had picked some of the youngest members of the student council to ask the mayor several key questions. The first was a little kindergarten girl, who raised her hand and said, "Mister Mayor, I know they want to put a bunch of stores in where the woods are now. But I don't understand something. There are lots of empty stores downtown. Why doesn't Mr. Beeks just make his new stores out of the old ones?"

The mayor looked annoyed, but said, "Well, young lady, Mr. Beeks can make the stores wherever he wants to. Wherever he builds them, they will create new jobs and prosperity for the good people of this town."

Then a first-grade boy asked, "But won't the new stores take away jobs, too? My daddy owns a butcher shop on Main Street, and he said that every time a bunch of stores goes up away from the center of town, it forces more downtown stores out of business."

Another little girl stood up and said, "My mom said the same thing about her bookstore."

A second boy stood up and said, "And what about traffic near our school? Right now, even with the woods behind it, crossing the streets is dangerous. Won't that get a lot worse if everybody is driving to the stores?"

The mayor held up his hands. "All right, children, thank you for your excellent questions. Our town is quite lucky to have such intelligent young citizens. But now question time is over, and the presentation will begin." I couldn't help but notice that he hadn't actually answered the last few questions, though.

Lizzie and I stepped up to the podium. Just as we had practiced a few days before, she gave a signal and the lights in the room dimmed. Lizzie took a deep breath, brought up the first slide, and began. The first several slides were photos and drawings of endangered local animals and their habitats. Lizzie went through the horrifying statistics on vanishing farmland and woodlands in our area, and explained how important it was to preserve the few remaining wooded areas within our town limits.

Mrs. Starsky looked excited. The student council kids were leaning forward in their seats nervously. I snuck a glance over toward the mayor, who was making a big show of yawning. I smiled. I had a feeling he wouldn't be yawning for long.

Next Lizzie presented a whole bunch of information that the student council members had put together about downtowns, and how important it was to the health of a city to have a successful central business area. She also showed pictures of several other towns in our area that had allowed developers to knock down all of their surrounding woodlands and put in huge stores. The downtowns were all horrible looking: empty sidewalks and row after row of boarded-up storefronts.

The mayor was still yawning, and one of the town council members was now doing a crossword puzzle.

For the final part of her presentation, Lizzie showed a bunch of photos we had taken of beautiful scenes in the forest, with happy student council members posing everywhere. As we had hoped, all the parents in the audience made "Awwww..." sounds every time a new slide of their children popped up. Lizzie ended this part of the program with a statement and a question: "We hear all the time that we children are the future. Well, don't we deserve a future that includes the beauty and magic of nature?"

All of the kids (except for James Beeks) and parents clapped wildly, while Mr. Beeks, the mayor, and the town council members just kind of sat there. As soon as the applause died down, the mayor stood up and said, "Thank you, children, for that heartfelt and touching presentation. Now I believe it is time for the council to take a vote on Mr. Beeks's permit application. Please know that we appreciate your participation and concern."

"Excuse me, sir?" I called out. "We're not finished yet. We've prepared extra information in case there are any questions from the council. We also have an expert witness available, if time allows."

I could tell the mayor was immensely annoyed, but he said, "Very well. Do we have any questions from the council?"

The member who had been working on the crossword said, "That was a lovely presentation.

However, I do have something I want to ask you: Are any of those animals you showed us officially listed as endangered in our area?"

Lizzie said, "Um, no. Not as far as I know, sir."

Then the same man asked, "And do you know for sure that each of those creatures actually lives on the specific piece of land that Mr. Beeks has purchased?"

"Um, no, sir."

Another council member, a woman with a big old-fashioned curly hairdo and pointy eyeglasses said, "Well, then, if you can't produce an actual example of an endangered species living in that particular area, I don't see how we can hold up Mr. Beeks's project."

I spoke up for the first time. "But we can. We were just waiting for our expert witness to present this part. Ladies and gentlemen, I present to you the world-famous wildlife expert, Dr. Rodger Chimpstone!"

This was where the leprechauns' magic became really important. They had used their illusion skills to make Rodger visible and human looking. He stepped forward amid polite applause and said, "The members of the student council first contacted me several weeks ago and asked me to investigate, look into, check out the status of the plant and animal life in the little forest we are discussing here today. As you have heard, there are many local species that need land like this to survive. However, I admit that we did not succeed in finding, locating, uncovering specimens of those animals here."

The mayor was smirking now.

"We found something even better, even more amazing, spectacular, and precious in your very own forest. Ladies and gentlemen, we found the first known living specimen of that rarest of amphibians: the Large-Mouthed Blue Frog!" Rodger reached into his jacket pocket and pulled out a familiar-looking blue creature. The leprechauns had used their magic to turn Dodger back into a frog for the evening. At first, Dodger hadn't wanted to go along with it, but then he had agreed—as long as we promised to give him some extra-juicy flies after the meeting.

Every person in the room was leaning forward to get a better look at Dodger, the Large-Mouthed Blue Frog. We had prepared for this, too. Lizzie turned on the webcam built into the computer and projected Dodger onto the big screen. Rodger continued his speech.

"This little fellow is unique, unmatched, alone in the world. He also has a distinctive cry and an incredible story." That was Dodger's cue.

"Du-u-ude!" he croaked. "Du-u-ude!"

Rodger said, "The Large-Mouthed Blue Frog is a faithful and loving creature. Because the species is so rare, the male will spend years and years hopping through the swamps, eating harmful and annoying insects and singing out with his mating call: Du-u-ude! Du-u-ude! He will carry on like this forever, or at least until he finds a female Large-Mouthed Blue Frog to be his lifelong companion, his love, his queen. Will you allow him to dream his patient dream of love and happiness, or will you chop down his home?"

The crowd was absolutely speechless. In the silence that followed, the mayor said, "Why don't we take a short recess break, and then come back to vote?" The lights came up around the room, and people started shuffling chairs around, going out of the room for drinks, and chatting with their neighbors.

Except for the kids. They all came rushing forward to play with Dodger. "Du-u-ude! Du-u-ude!" he cried happily. Dodger always loves attention.

Meanwhile, Lizzie called the mayor over. He frowned but made his way across the front of the room to us. Mrs. Starsky must have sensed trouble brewing, because she came scurrying in our direction as well. "Sir," Lizzie said to the mayor, "I would like to ask you to abstain from voting."

"Abstain? Why in the world would I abstain, little girl?"

"Well, it's just that . . . I don't think you can possibly be a fair judge in this issue."

He put on his big, fake smile and said, "I can't imagine what you're talking about. I love the environment as much as anybody, and—"

"No, you don't!" Lizzie said under her breath. It was time for the fireworks to start.

"Excuse me, young lady. Did you just interrupt me? And did you dare to stand here and claim that I do not love the environment?"

Lizzie stood her ground. "I did. Because you don't!"

"That's a lie!" the mayor growled.

"Really?" Lizzie asked. Then she turned off the projector screen, faced the screen of the computer in the mayor's direction, opened up the video from his visit to our school, and pressed PLAY. Boy, the mayor didn't look very attractive when he was ranting and raving in close-up: "I came here because you wanted to save the forest and preserve the environment. Well, you know what? Nobody elected me to protect a bunch of trees! I couldn't care less about the environment! If it would help the most prominent citizens of this town to make money, I'd go out there and chop down those stupid trees myself!"

Jeepers. The mayor leaned toward Lizzie and hissed, "This is blackmail, and I won't stand for it! Give me that computer!"

"Not so fast," Mrs. Starsky said, stepping between the mayor and Lizzie. "That computer and everything on it is school property. And if Lizzie wants to, I think she could show that clip to the whole audience after the break. After all, you said it on public property, in a public meeting. Surely you aren't trying to say that showing these words to the public would be blackmail?"

The mayor stormed away, but when the meeting started again, he excused himself from voting. There was only one other thing to say before the vote was cast, and it was my job to say it. "Excuse me," I said, "I have a proposal that I think the council should hear before voting." I had come up with this part all by myself after reading my father's Step Eight: Make a Win-Win Plan. At first, I hadn't been sure exactly what making a win-win plan was, but then I had realized it was exactly what I had done when I'd negotiated with my mom for the right to go downtown to Lasorda's office. And again when we had worked together with the leprechauns. How cool was that? I was learning how to get what I wanted, and make other people happy, too!

Anyway, I took a deep breath and began.

"I have thought really hard about this, and I believe there might be a way to make everybody happy. The seller of the land, Mr. Lasorda, wants money to pay off his debts. The buyer, Mr. Beeks, wants a place to open up his funplex, which sounds like an excellent project. The town wants jobs for its citizens. And the student council wants to preserve the forest lands for our future. Am I correct?"

I looked up from my paper and saw nods all around. Of course, my win-win plan went even further. I had an idea for how the Great Lasorda and Dodger could work things out with each other and the leprechauns, too, but I wasn't about to announce that part at a town council meeting. First I had to save the forest.

"Now, it has come to my attention that the town owns a whole square block of abandoned storefront real estate right on Main Street. What I propose is this: Why can't Mr. Beeks pay Mr. Lasorda for the forest, but then swap pieces of land with the town and build his project in the downtown location? That will be great for business AND great for the environment. Mr. Lasorda will get paid, Mr. Beeks will get a place to build his businesses, the town will get a newer, better Main Street, and the forest will be saved for the Large-Mouthed Blue Frog. What do you think?"

The entire room erupted in muttering. I heard shouts from all over the room:

"Outrageous!"

"Who does this kid think he is?"

"Excellent! I think this boy should be our next mayor!"

"Up with frogs!"

Right in front of me, I saw James Beeks say to his father, "Dad, I hate to say it, but I think Willie's idea is really good!"

Then Mr. Beeks whispered back, "You don't understand—Beeks, Beeks, Beeks, and Son never backs down. And we never lose!"

James replied, "It isn't losing if everybody winds up happy. It's just good business." Mr. Beeks looked stunned for a moment, but then—slowly, slowly—he smiled at his son.

When the noise died down, the president of the town council asked Mr. Beeks if he would be satisfied with the new arrangement. I held my breath, but after a moment, Mr. Beeks nodded. The members of the council whispered to each other frantically for a while, but then announced that they would now vote on my proposal.

I never would have believed it before, but politics can be kind of exciting.

CHAPTER SEVENTEEN

The Beeks, Beeks, Beeks, and Son Blue Frog Preserve

LET ME TELL YOU how things turned out. The vote passed. The leprechauns turned Dodger back into himself, so Lizzie didn't even have to kiss him to break the frog spell. Beeks, Beeks, Beeks, and Son traded the forest to the town in exchange for the square block of valuable downtown real estate. The town promised to leave the forest undeveloped forever, and named the area the Beeks, Beeks, Beeks, and Son Blue Frog Preserve. The Great Lasorda got to keep the money he got for selling the forest. The leprechauns got a free, safe place to live. The student council got a huge blue plaque from the mayor and the town council. Mrs. Starsky was really, really proud. I have a feeling she didn't erase the webcam recording, though—just in case.

And that's not all. Amy got to keep her title as Queen of the Leprechauns. That might not seem like much, but it comes with some cool benefits. Here's the best one: Every once in a while, when Amy runs a little short on cash, she leaves a pair of shoes under her bed. And I'm not going to tell you that the leprechauns fill her shoes with fairy gold or anything—that would just be too crazy. But all I know is that I have the only little sister in town who can afford her own state-of-the-art detective lab. Plus some pocket money for ice cream.

The Great Lasorda is doing all right, too. He argued and complained a lot about having to share his forest with the leprechauns for all eternity, but really, I think that ever since everybody stopped arguing about who owes what, he and his new partners, Rodger and Dodger, enjoy the company.

Speaking of company, one day in early spring, I was walking home alone through the forest, and suddenly found that James Beeks was walking along next to me. "You know," he said, "I guess you and Lizzie were right: The woods are kind of cool after all." There was a red-and-white fast-food bag blocking the path in front of us, and Beeks started to step around it. Then he looked at me sheepishly, bent over, and picked up the bag. "Still," he said, "having my own private place to practice baseball would have been awesome."

That was when I got a crazy idea. It was nutty to even think about, because Beeks and I had always been enemies. But on the other hand, he had kind of helped us to save the forest. And he had admitted Lizzie and I were right about something. And he had even picked up trash in the woods without being ordered to. Before I could think twice, I said, "You know, James, I know a field where we can practice baseball all we want."

He looked at me like I had suddenly grown a pair of bug antennae from my head. "You mean, together?"

I nodded.

"Really?"

I nodded again.

He thought this over and said, "Is the field any good?"

I didn't reply, because I didn't have to. I just turned down the little side path that led to the Field of Dreams. James might have muttered a little under his breath, but he followed me. When we broke out of the trees and into the clearing, he looked around in awe. "How—" he started to ask.

"It's a really long story, James."

Beeks rubbed his eyes, looked around again, and said, "And this is really all yours?"

"And yours, whenever you need a place to work out. I mean, if you want to. We could get ready for the season together."

"I guess I can give it a try," James said. "But, um, does this mean we're, like, friends?"

"Believe me," I said, "stranger things have been known to happen." With that, I walked over to the equipment locker behind the backstop and threw him a glove. He caught it and smiled.

Lizzie and I are still best friends, of course. She's trying to convince me to run for president of the sixth grade when we get to middle school. I tell her we'll see what happens. But she knows as well as I do that I'll probably give in.

My dad is still waiting for my book notes about the quest to save the forest. I told him I'm still polishing them up, but that I'll let him know when they're ready for the world to read them.

Yeah, right.

In the meantime, if you aren't sure you believe me about all of this, you can come visit the Beeks, Beeks, Beeks, and Son Blue Frog Preserve. If you're brave enough, and your heart is pure enough, you can start picking up any pieces of litter you see there. Then, if you listen very, very carefully, you might just be lucky enough to hear the strange sound of the blue frog calling out to his missing queen: *Du-u-ude! Du-u-ude!*

Or maybe that's just Dodger playing baseball.